AWAKE IN THE NIGHT

SHAUNA MC ELENEY

CONTENT WARNING

This book contains material that may be triggering for some readers. If you feel a content warning isn't necessary for you, or may spoil your enjoyment of the story, then feel free to skip the below.

CW: incidents of suicide (on page); mentions of self-harm, child death, back street abortion, homophobia, discussions of mental health issues and alcohol abuse.

For my parents John and Marian.
Thank you for always giving me a place to land.

AWAKE IN THE NIGHT

PROLOGUE

There's blood in my mouth.

There's blood in my mouth, and I don't know why, but there's too much to swallow. It's filling my windpipe: I'm coughing, trying to breathe, but the blood splutters out anyway, choking me. I can't see him anywhere, I don't know where he's gone, but there's a sharp pain in my throat now, a stabbing pain.

Let them get away. Please, God, let them get away.

I can't breathe, and everything tastes... wrong, too thick and too heavy in my throat, like I'm choking on a bag of pennies. I reach up to touch it, and it feels wet – the skin across the windpipe ragged, already parting.

I can't do it, I can't stand up anymore. I need to sit, to breathe.

A hand on my stomach, over the baby, and I remember I *can't* fall, mustn't. I need to stay upright. Need to protect the baby.

I can hear him shuffling, just behind me. I turn around and he's in front of me, white shirt soaked in blood. I look down at my hands and dress, then back at him.

My blood. It's my blood soaking him.

Another sharp pain, low in my stomach, and oh God, she's coming, the baby's coming. I crash down to my knees, coughing and gasping, red blood spreading out from me across the white tile. There's too much, like a tin of red paint knocked over an altar.

Because you're dying.

My eyes are closing. I can't stop them.

It's dark, but I'm not afraid of the dark.

There are hands on me, dragging me. I try to speak, but I can't – my mouth won't open, nor my eyes. It's cold, and I'm tired. I need to rest.

Maybe I should.

I'm not afraid, though. I'm not afraid of the dark.

CHAPTER 1

2018

The Kia Rondo turned onto the quiet street, passing eight houses before pulling up to the curb outside the house: number 17 Montpellier Street. It needed painting, its state of comparative disrepair distinguishing it unhappily from its neighbours. A large weeping willow tree stood in the garden, looming dangerously close to the left side of the building – protecting or threatening it, depending on the day.

The house was different in other ways, too. The front door was wider, with a grand set of steps leading up to it from the pavement; a shepherd, looking watchfully down on his flock. Where the other houses made do with low white walls, number 17 was ringed by iron fencing, fully fortified against intruders – the high steel gates plugging the single gap in the fence the only means by which a visitor might enter the drive.

Montpellier Street as a whole was modest: little space separated one detached property from another, and most homes offered their residents only three or four small bedrooms. Number 17, however, had six, supplemented by an attic and, unusually for Galway, a basement – though both, like the house itself, were in dire need of restoration.

For the women in the Kia, number 17's newest owner-occupiers, this restoration had become a kind of mission. The house was dying, or perhaps it was dead already, but they planned to revive it: to paint the walls, open every window, fill the kitchen with the smell of cooking and make it a home. Their forever home, ideally.

"How did moving day and the warmest day of the year align? How?" Nicole turned to look at her wife – who was, as always, busy sticking her camera out of the window to photograph the house.

Jessica carried her camera with her everywhere; no matter that it was 2018 and she had a camera on her phone. A camera-phone wasn't the same as an SLR, she argued, and would not be moved on the topic. Nicole had begun calling her Cyclops early on in their relationship, because it felt like every time she turned around, Jess's face was nothing but a lens framed by short brown hair - and, though she loved Jess's passion for photography, a part of her hated the way it deprived her of the sight of her wife's beautiful hazel eyes.

"Sweetheart, you're from Melbourne," Jess told her. "You should be able to hack this. So suck it up." She finished with a playful punch to Nicole's arm.

"I've acclimatised! But fine - let's get into it, if we have to. The moving van should be here in like half an hour. We can unpack the car and get everything inside before the bigger stuff arrives."

"A sound plan." Jessica grinned. "Have you seen who's back over the fence, by the way?" she added. "Bags not talking to her!"

Nicole glanced out of the car window and saw a woman peering, in a none-too subtle fashion, in their direction. It was their new neighbour and, though they hadn't spoken to her yet, they'd seen her on their two previous visits to the property. She was short, with a shock of grey curly hair - the first thing you saw, when you looked at her.

"Why do I have to talk to her?" Nicole pulled up to the right-hand side of the house and turned off the engine. "We should go *together*, introduce ourselves. It's what people do."

"Yes, but you're the social butterfly, and I can't be arsed. Plus! You can casually mention your wife and feel out any homophobic vibes, so when we rip out the fencing, we'll know in advance how high to make the wall."

Jessica hopped out of the side of the car closest to the house and left Nicole to exit right beside the neighbour. The curly-haired woman had now made her way over to the Kia driver's door – Nicole saw there was no way out.

"Good morning there! You must be our new neighbour."

The woman sounded friendly, chirpy even. Up close, Nicole could see she had a warm, open face, with a smile that revealed a set of crooked teeth, overlapped slightly and crowding the front of her mouth. The curly hair was short, and she had blue eyes that were right then making their way up and down Nicole and the car.

"I'm Susan, Susan Devlin. You're so very welcome to Montpellier Street."

She had a soft accent, clear and with only a little lilt; a Galway one, Nicole thought, with none of the hard edges she'd come to associate with Limerick and Dublin. She was used to Irish accents, after ten years of living in the country, but sometimes she still came up against someone who might as well have been speaking in actual Irish for all she could understand.

"Thank you. Nicole Taylor - it's a pleasure to meet you." Nicole stuck her hand through the fence and Susan shook it gently on the other side.

"Oh! Well now, you're not a local anyways, are you? Not with that accent." Susan was still holding Nicole's hand.

"No, I'm Australian, but I've been here ten years so...honorary Irish?"

"Not yet love, but we'll let you know." Susan finally relinquished Nicole's hand. "You must hate the weather here! What part of Australia are you from? I have a nephew out there now... Perth, I think it is. 'Tis great for them to get away travelling, isn't it, though? There was none of that when I was their age, I can tell you!"

Susan talked a mile a minute. Nicole wondered if this was what she did all day: just stood in her garden, waiting for people to pass so she could pounce on them.

I wonder if she lives alone?

"I'm from Melbourne, a place called Kensington." She interrupted eventually. "I'm well used to the weather here now though. Rain and more rain, especially on the West Coast. It's not called the Wild Atlantic Way for nothing, I guess. But what about you, Susan? You a local?"

"Oh, I am, love - born and raised on Montpellier Street, I never left the place. I live here now with my husband Billy. Our boy Michael's long gone out of the house, but he only lives round the corner, so he calls into us a good bit. He's single by the way," she added, winking. "Has his own business too – he's an electrician. Are you married yourself, love, or are you moving in alone? It's an awful big house to live in alone, if you don't mind me saying - there must be six bedrooms in there. I'm not sure what way they have it laid out now, but it's seen a few changes over the years. A lot of people have come and gone from number seventeen, so they have."

How necessary *was* she to the conversation at this point, Nicole pondered as the older woman talked on? She felt quietly confident that, if she backed away, Susan might not even notice she'd gone.

"I'm married, actually," she said eventually, finally getting in an answer to Susan's endless questions. "So it'll be me and my wife whipping this place into shape." She couldn't help but try to gauge Susan's reaction to this disclosure as she spoke – it was habitual, these days – but she battled on regardless. "There are six rooms at the moment, I believe, but one is the attic and another the basement, so we won't use those as bedrooms, I guess. Lots to do, anyway."

"Oh, how wonderful! Lesbians!" Susan beamed at Nicole. "My friend Margret's sister has a daughter in college up in Dublin, and she's friends with a lesbian."

She sounded rather pleased to have been able to identify one in her own life, albeit at several degrees' distance.

"Okay, well...that's great." Nicole saw the opportunity for an exit present itself in the split-second lull in conversation Susan's precipitated, and she seized it with both hands. "I'd better be getting in - we have so much unpacking to do. But it's been great to meet you." She began to walk towards the house; a clear signal, she hoped, of her intention to head inside.

"Best of luck to you Nicole, to you and..."

"Jessica. Jessica Murphy."

"Jessica! Lovely. We must have you round for tea when you're all settled."

"Sure, let's do that."

Her back turned on Susan, she walked up the steps to the front door, turned the handle to open it, and found it locked. *Weird.* She reached into the pocket of her and pulled out the key. The door was unusually large; it had been one of the first things to catch Nicole's eye when they viewed the house the first time. It was painted green but, like the white of the walls around the doorway, the green was peeling. She brushed her hand along the paint and watched as it came away and fell floating to the step below; unlocked the door and pushed it open, stepping over the threshold and forward, until she was standing in the hallway of her new home.

"Jess? Jess, where are you?" The house sounded painfully empty, her own voice an echo.

There was no response. She went left into the main living room, saw it was unoccupied, then came back out and down the hall into the kitchen. Light flooded in through the window over the sink there, but only served to show up the dust on every surface. A musty smell hung in all the rooms, and Nicole longed to open the windows and let the billowing salty winds of the Atlantic cleanse the house for their new start. Their *fresh* start.

Jess was still nowhere to be seen. Nicole wandered back up the hall, this time taking a left into the other living area: a slightly smaller, more intimate room with a fireplace and the same high ceilings and original cornices as the other rooms of the house. She scanned the room; was about to walk right back out again when she spotted Jess at the bay window, reading a book on the built-in seat that looked out onto the street outside.

She was a compulsive reader; Nicole loved that about her, too. She could get lost in a book for hours, sometimes days. Sci-fi, fantasy and horror were her go-tos, though it was Terry Pratchett's Discworld series she returned to when she most needed comfort. She loved Pratchett, had loved him since childhood; would reach for one of his books when she was anxious, whenever something was playing on her mind.

She was a slight woman, Jess; so slight that when she curled her legs up under herself, she became tiny, so lost in the room Nicole almost didn't even notice she was there.

"There you are." Nicole was flooded, unexpectedly, with relief at having found her. "Babe, why didn't you answer me? And why did you lock me out? First you leave me to the mercy of our *very* chatty neighbour, and then you bolt me out of my own house."

"Sorry. I was miles away, I didn't hear you. And I didn't touch the door, so that's strange. We should check to see if the lock needs replacing."

"Well, the neighbour seems lovely, anyway. Her name's Susan. I mentioned I have a wife and I think we're okay to keep the low wall for the extra light like we talked about. She even managed to identify a lesbian in her own life, which was delightful. Also, how do you have a book? I note you have moved *nothing* from the car yet."

Jess didn't even look up. "You know my motto, never leave home without a book—"

"—in your handbag," Nicole finished for her. "Yes, I know. I love you."

Jessica rested the book in her lap and tilted her head up and out towards the window. The light caught her face and she closed her eyes to the glare. "I know. I love you too."

CHAPTER 2

1955

The four-door Fiat 1100 turned onto the quiet street, passing eight houses before pulling up to the curb outside the house: number 17, Montpellier Street. From the back seat, Grace gazed out the window, much as she had the entire journey; she rarely travelled by car, and was always slightly mesmerised by the passing houses and trees as they blurred together, by the hum of the engine that shuttered through her body and threatened to send her to sleep. The driver's door opened, but she stayed where she was - looking out at the large house, which contained what seemed like a workforce of people, all busying themselves around the grounds. The building stood taller than the ones around it and was painted a bright, blinding white; it almost hurt her eyes to look directly at it. Steps led up to a big wooden door, its green gloss as wet as water; a large weeping willow grew outside, hanging dangerously close to the left side of the house. She was taking it all in, inventorying it through the ink black bars of the iron fence, when her own door was abruptly opened.

"Well? Get out, child!" Sister Mary Agnes Fitzgerald stood directly outside the Fiat, peering in at Grace. "What are you waiting for? Now!"

Sister Fitzgerald was the Mother Superior, back at the home for girls that was her current residence. Grace had been placed there when she was fourteen, after both of her parents – and her younger brothers, one ten and the other seven – were killed in a fire at the family farm, leaving her with no place to go; she was coming up now on her two-year anniversary. The circumstances of her placement marked her as different from the other girls: most of them were unmarried mothers, pregnant out of wedlock and disowned by their families.

The nun, from Grace's perspective at least, was a formidable woman. She was in her early fifties, with jet black hair - not that you often saw it under the tight-fitting coif she wore in public, complemented by a veil and habit. She stood, as she always stood, with her shoulders back, adding an extra inch to her 5'8". Grace, at only 5'2", couldn't help but be intimidated. Moreover, Sister Fitzgerald was strict in the extreme: all the girls were petrified of her, and even some of the younger nuns. At times, her strictness extended to the meting-out of physical discipline: when, for example, Grace was caught up in a daydream and didn't hear the dinner bell, or was slow to get in line when returning from the yard, Sister Fitzgerald would grab her by the hair and *pull* her along by it, leaving Grace with a stinging, tear-inducing pain in her scalp that lasted long after she was released.

No one wanted to get on the wrong side of Sister Fitzgerald. The trouble was, Grace thought, Sister Fitzgerald didn't have a *right* side. Making yourself invisible was the key to surviving around her.

Grace had seen enough of her to be sure of that.

"This is your new home," the nun had bellowed from the top of the hall as the girls filed in. "You will treat it with respect – more respect than you have shown yourselves, thus far. *Melius erit*, girls. *Melius erit.*"

There was an assembly every morning at the home, but the big speeches were reserved for those days that saw the arrival of a new batch of girls - girls, and women, their ages ranging everywhere from 12 to 29. Grace had seen dozens of them come and go in the last two years. A lot of them entered pregnant, but few of them ever left with a child: St. Brigid's Home for Girls was proud of its successful adoption rates. There were rumours that not all the mothers actually *wanted* their children adopted - but no one talked much about that.

As Sister Fitzgerald had given her speech and listed out her beloved rules and regulations, Grace had let her attention wander around the main hall. Her eye had been caught by a girl around her own age and height; she had long brown hair, but Grace couldn't see her face. The girl's head was bowed, and she'd looked scared.

Over the next few days, Grace had made it her business to get to know the shy girl she'd spied in the hall – whose name, she'd learned, was Ellen. She was 16, like Grace, and, also like Grace, was in the home because she was an orphan. Her mother had died of tuberculosis ten years before, in 1945, leaving Ellen's father to raise her and her younger brother - but he was an alcoholic who'd never recovered from his wife's death, and he'd drunk himself into an early grave. Ellen's brother Eoin was sent off to live in England with their uncle, who had land, and who took Eoin on to help him farm it. Ellen was of no interest to him, however, so it was left to the nuns of St. Brigid's to take her in.

Grace, for reasons she'd not quite understood, had felt compelled to protect Ellen; perhaps, she'd reasoned, because Ellen had already endured so much hardship, and Grace was desperate to steer her away from suffering more. Every day, in between working in the laundry, saying prayers and performing the other duties that formed the St. Brigid's girls' daily routine, Grace would seek her out, and eventually Ellen had responded in kind, until all their free time was spent together. Grace's favourite times of the week were Tuesday and Thursday mornings when, at 11am sharp, they'd attend choir practice: standing close to one another as they sang their hymns, their shoulders occasionally pressing together.

It was on one of those Tuesday mornings that Grace had discovered Ellen could play the piano.

They were standing around the choir room as usual, overseen by Sister Tabitha - the youngest nun at St. Brigit's at only twenty-one, and so young-looking she could have passed, without the habit, as another of the girls in the home. Everyone liked her: she was never mean, and was one of the only staff members to treat the girls with some dignity, asking them about their backgrounds and their plans for the future as if they were people as real as her.

"Good morning, ladies, and welcome," she'd said. "First things first: can any of the new arrivals play an instrument?" She'd cast a glance around the room and waited, expectantly, for a reply. "Come along, don't be shy."

To Grace's surprise, Ellen had raised her hand high in the air.

"I can play the piano," she'd said, her tone surprisingly assured.

"Marvellous!" Sister Tabitha had enthused. "Come on down here and take a seat." She'd pointed, then, at the tiny stool half-hidden under the piano in the corner of the room.

Ellen had made her way down through the throng of girls to the front, where she'd taken her seat as requested. Grace had watched her move, and felt suddenly enamoured of this newfound confidence in her friend. As Ellen had started to play, the mood in the room had changed: everyone looking up from their feet or their hands, their eyes on Ellen. Her nimble fingers had moved effortlessly across the ivory keys, and she'd seemed at one with the piano, letting her body move and sway in time with the music. The melody she made filled the room and, for a moment, there'd been a lightness, a joy. Ellen's green eyes had been closed as she'd given herself up to the music; but when, occasionally, they'd opened, they'd seemed to sparkle. She'd looked... happy, and the hair on Grace's arms had risen up as she'd gazed on in a kind of awe.

Later that afternoon, Ellen and Grace had been working in the laundry:
a large industrial affair, with linen coming in from hotels and guesthouses
all around Galway. The dirty linen was unloaded in big blue cloth bags, then
dragged through to the back warehouse. The girls were tasked with pulling
the bags into the laundry area, where their contents were washed, dried and
steam-ironed before being folded and packed back into the same big blue
bags, to be returned whence they came.

Ellen and Grace had been working together in one of the back rooms. By
the time the laundry got to them there, it was already washed and dried; their
job had been to run it through the big rollers, where it was steamed before
being left to cool. This had been two days on from the piano revelation, and
Grace was making fun of Ellen.

"I just had no idea I was in the presence of such grrreatness." Grace threw
her arms up in the air, before taking an exaggerated bow. Ellen, in turn, had
burst into laughter at the performance and slapped her hand over her mouth
to try to stifle her laughter. It had been too late, though, and she'd let out a
massive snort which had only egged Grace on more: thereafter, Grace had
proceeded to waltz around the steam room and, when a puff of steam had
shot up into the air, she'd parted it with her hands, as if walking on stage
through a cloud of smoke. The act was too much for Ellen, who'd kept on
laughing uncontrollably – and who'd been laughing, still, when Sister Mary
Agnes Fitzgerald had stepped into the laundry.

"What in under God is going on in here?" the nun had roared as she'd
come upon them, the steam hissing as it escaped into the air around her. It
was as if a dragon had entered the room, spitting fire.

Ellen had tried to calm the situation. "Sister Mary, we were just working.
Grace said something funny, is all."

"What did you call me, child?" There'd been an unsettling calmness in
the nun's voice that had verged on eerie.

You can only call her Sister Fitzgerald: Grace had willed Ellen to pick up on the thought, to apologise and correct her mistake, but had known, deep down, it was too late.

And her fears had been realised when Sister Fitzgerald had walked, still unnaturally calm, over to Ellen, coming to a stop only inches from her face.

"What did you call me, girl?" she'd repeated.

"Sister...sis..." Ellen had frozen, paralysed with dread. Steam continued to hiss around them, the nozzles pointing down towards the wrinkled fabric and periodically spewing forth white heat – the sound of it rhythmic, hypnotic.

5,4,3,2,1 HISS... 5,4,3,2,1 HISS...

Sister Fitzgerald had taken Ellen's wrist gently in her hand, as if to examine it.

"I hear you play the piano, child. Quite beautifully, by all accounts."

Her soft tone had been unbearable. Ellen had remained silent, unable to speak; *staying* silent even when Sister Fitzgerald had brought her hand – and Ellen's – to rest under the vent.

5,4...

"I'm so sorry, Sister Fitzgerald... I didn't mean any disrespect," Ellen had stammered, her eyes fixed on their conjoined hands.

3,2...

"You must learn respect, child. And we are here to teach you, to help you."

1.

The scream had been horrendous: seeming to last longer than it possibly could have, and giving Grace the impression that time had stopped entirely. It had reverberated around the room, and Sister Fitzgerald had been forced to wrap a second hand around Ellen's wrist to hold her in place as she'd resisted, tried to pull away from the boiling jets.

What happened next was, at least for Grace, a blur. Later, she'd remember the feeling of rage that had overwhelmed her as she'd grabbed Sister Fitzgerald's hand and yanked it away from the jets, Ellen's wrist still firmly seized within it. She'd remember the smell – would never *forget* the smell of skin simmering on the bone, the flesh already raised and blistered and peeling back from the nimble fingers that had glided up and down the keys of the old piano. She'd also remember the look on Sister Fitzgerald's face when she grabbed her, the look of disbelief, and the relief on Ellen's when she saw her wrist was free. One of the last things Grace would remember was her own pain: the pain she'd felt across the side of her head as the 'wedding ring' on Sister Fitzgerald's right hand met the soft tissue of her temple, and the duller pain when she'd fallen back against the cement floor.

And then... nothing.

Grace had woken two days later in the infirmary, Sister Tabitha by her side as she came awake. She'd spent several days there - but it had been tolerable, because Ellen had been there too, having her own wounds treated. Kind, gentle Sister Tabitha had been their main carer.

On the third day, Sister Fitzgerald had appeared at Grace's bedside.

"You are feeling better, my child, after your dizzy spell." It hadn't been a question; there'd been no need for Grace to respond.

"Tomorrow morning, I need you down at the front door, 7am sharp. You are to be part of a new project, and you'll be staying in a brand-new house. Don't worry," she'd added, glancing across at Ellen, asleep in the next bed, "it's only the street over, Montpellier Street. So you won't be far from your... *friend*."

"**C**ome along child, we don't have all day." Sister Fitzgerald reached in and grabbed Grace's wrist as she'd once grabbed Ellen's, yanking her from the back of the car.

Grace stood, and followed the woman in black along the short drive and up the steps that led up to the big, wide wooden door. The house looked beautiful; perhaps, she thought, Sister Fitzgerald felt bad about what had happened in the steam room, and this relocation to the new house was her way of making amends?

She crossed the threshold; couldn't help but run her fingers over the door's bright green gloss. The paint, still wet to the touch, smudged under her fingertips; Sister Fitzgerald, seeing this, slapped her hand away from the door with an almighty wallop.

"Must you destroy everything you touch?" she said, her voice low and spiteful.

Grace rubbed her middle and index finger together; watched as the paint became tacky between them, then flaked away and fell onto the step below.

CHAPTER 3

2018

Nicole was in the kitchen unpacking the groceries when she felt Jessica come up behind her, wrap her arms around Nicole's waist and lean into her back.

"Hi," she mumbled, from somewhere in Nicole's shoulders.

"Hi," Nicole said. Then: "How am I so lucky, that I get to have you?"

"I don't know, but I'm yours now." Jessica rose up on her tiptoes and kissed the back of Nicole's neck, before pulling away; walked across to one of the shopping bags and began to root around in it. "I'm going to start dinner. Where's the mince?"

"Are you sure it's not there?" Nicole craned her neck to peer into the open bag. "I could have sworn I picked it up."

"Nope. Definitely not in here."

"Crap. Okay, I'll go back, it won't take long." Nicole snatched up the keys and headed for the door. "I'll be right back. It's worth going to get it – we can't have spaghetti Bolognese without mince."

"Oh, hold up! Sorry babe, it's here in the other bag." Jessica held the Styrofoam pack of minced meat up in front of her face, sheepish.

Nicole dropped the keys back on the table and rolled her eyes. "You're lucky you're pretty. Blind, but pretty." She made her way back over to Jessica; wrapped an arm around her waist and pulled her close. "Can you believe we live here?"

Jessica smiled back against her neck. "Welcome home."

"Oh, you know what we should do?" Nicole asked, pointing her half empty wine glass at her wife as they stacked the dishwasher after dinner.

"What?" Jess's response had a tinge of trepidation at the edges. She eyed Nic, then the wine glass, its contents already splashing at the rim of the glass.

"We should check out the attic."

"Oh, that feels like a daytime thing, doesn't it? A bright, sober daytime thing."

But Nicole was already closing the dishwasher - and opening the kitchen drawer where the key to the attic was kept. They hadn't been able to gain access to it when they'd viewed the property: the first time they asked, they'd been told the pulldown stairs were broken but due to be replaced before the sale was finalised, and the next time no one had been able to find the key for the lock. The estate agent had shown them blueprints for the attic, though, and they knew there was a window up there, because they could see it from outside the house. They also knew it was fully wired, and had been used as a bedroom before, so imagined at the time they might utilise it in the future for a study, or something similar.

Nicole stretched her 5'8" frame to its full height below the hatch leading up to the attic, but was still nowhere near the handle. Jess watched her from the door frame of one of the bedrooms, eyebrow raised.

"Really, you thought you were reaching that? How much wine have you had?"

"Hey, we're sharing the bottle - I'm only one ahead of you." Nicole paused, a solution occurring to her. "Oh! The stick thingy." She reached into the little closet door that held the water tank and pulled out a wooden stick with a hook on the end – designed, they'd been told, for looping into the handle of the hatch. She steadied herself; threaded the hook through the loop and yanked the stairs down. The steps unfolded in three parts, coming to rest at her feet and inviting her to venture upwards, into the small dark rectangle that now hovered above her.

"Okay," said Jess. "But one more time, just for the record - I'm not loving this idea."

"It's fine - you worry too much. Besides, what's the wo—"

"Don't you say it!"

"—rst that can happen?" Nicole finished, sticking out her tongue and making her way up the ladder.

"Turn on the light!"

"Yes, thank you, I'm looking for it." Fumbling in the darkness, Nicole grabbed for the pull cord, which she batted against her hand for a moment like a playful cat. "Oh, for fuck's sakes... Okay! Got it!"

She pulled on the cord and the upper floor brightened, revealing three dim light bulbs hanging naked in a row leading from the hatch entrance to the round window on the far side of the gable. The space was completely empty but for a rocking chair, which sat directly under the middle bulb, as if someone had placed it there deliberately.

"Well, that looks creepy as," Jess murmured from behind her.

"It's just a rocking chair. That's not creepy, it's...totally fine."

"Yeah, a lone rocking chair in an old, unfurnished house. Fine, totally fine."

"I'm going to sit in it. Wait back here."

Nicole strode determinedly into the centre of the attic, towards the rocker.

"Wait back here? What do you think it's going to do? I'm coming with you."

Jessica followed her across the room, until they stood one on either side of the chair.

"You going to sit in it?" Jess asked.

"Nope. You?" Nicole's eyes were glued to the chair.

"Nope. We could sell it?"

"That sounds like a plan. We can move it tomorrow when it's bright out. You wanna get out of here?"

"100%"

They took the stairs quickly.

"So," Nicole said, when they were halfway down the landing, "the attic might be more of a daytime space..."

Nicole woke up with a start. She reached out across the bed for Jessica, but found nothing; reached further, until she was almost touching the end of the mattress. The bed was empty. "Jessica?"

She picked up her phone and activated the flashlight, illuminating the bedroom and its meagre furnishings: a king size bed, a dresser on the far wall, and ten large cardboard boxes, all yet to be unpacked. There was no sign of Jessica anywhere. She got out of the bed and walked onto the landing; a little unsteady, she noticed, on her feet.

Christ, how much wine did I drink?

She could hear something. A noise: something faint she couldn't decipher that might have been coming from above her or below. A gentle rhythmic clank of wood on wood, suggestive of a rocking motion. Her breath caught in her chest, and against her better judgement, she looked up. The attic hatch was unlocked: closed, but unlocked.

"Jessica?" she said, as loudly as she dared, afraid of who could be up there, if not her wife.

Get a hold of yourself.

She looked around in the darkness, struggling to see anything in the faint light bleeding through the bathroom window. As her eyes began to adjust, she saw something on the ground: the wooden pole with the hook, lying directly below the attic entrance.

Fuck, fuck, fuck.

She picked up the pole and reached up, latching the hook into the loop as she had before and pulling open the hatch. Again, the stairs unfolded down to her; the sound of the rocking increased, but the rhythm was unchanged, its pace and pitch undisturbed by the opening of the attic. "Jessica? Jess, are you up there? This is really not funny!"

She stepped onto the ladder and made a slow ascent to the top; poked her head over the hatch and looked down the length of the attic space, unable to reach the cord for the lightbulb without climbing in further. The moon, at least, provided a modicum of light - streaming in, albeit weakly, through the round window on the far wall. She waited a moment for her eyes to adjust a second time, then saw, as they focused, the rocking chair in the centre of the room, and Jess cocooned inside it: moving back and forth, back and forth, seemingly oblivious to Nicole's arrival. "Jessica - what the actual fuck? You scared the shit out of me!"

"Nic? Nic, is that...is that you?" Jessica's voice was low, broken. She didn't move, didn't turn her head or stop her rocking.

"What are you doing up here?" Nicole didn't know if she was angry or frightened by the sight of her wife and the chair. "Couldn't you sleep? Why didn't you wake me?"

She pulled herself through the hatch and into the room.

Jessica stopped rocking; stood up and turned to face Nicole. "Hi." Her voice was breaking, now. "You're here."

"Are you okay?" Nicole took a couple of steps forward. "Babe, are you okay?"

Jessica shuffled towards her, bridging the gap between them. As the angles of her body shifted, the moonlight hit her face, illuminating her features.

Her eyes were gone.

Nicole recoiled, horrified, her right hand shooting up to her mouth to stifle the gasp rising up from her throat. "Your eyes! Jesus, Jess, what's wrong with your eyes?"

In every other respect, Jessica's face looked as it always did – her smile perfect, beatific. But her eyes – her eyes were missing, two black voids occupying the space where they should've been.

Nicole closed her own eyes; brought the heel of both hands up to them and pressed down until it hurt a little. When she took her hands away, everything was blurred – every object in her field of vision, Jessica included.

Jessica was closer now, her arm extended towards Nicole. Nicole blinked again as she felt Jess's hand touch her shoulder. There was something in the air up here, a burning smell. She breathed it in; opened her mouth to taste it.

"Nic?"

Nicole looked back at Jessica, her nose and lips and smile. Her hazel eyes, restored. Back, as if they'd never been gone.

"Jess, what are you doing up here?"

"I don't know." The reply came as a whisper. "I don't remember, I don't remember how I got up here. But *you're* here." She smiled and reached her arms around Nicole's neck. "You're *here*."

"You smell like talcum powder," Nicole said, the words half muffled by Jessica's skin.

"You smell like you," Jessica told her.

"Babe, you're freezing." Nicole rubbed her hands up and down Jessica's back. "Let's go back to bed?"

"To bed?" Jessica pulled back, but kept her arms around Nicole.

"Yes, to bed. It's 3am and I think you might be sleepwalking again. God, you haven't done that since college, you remember?"

Jessica was staring at Nicole, she stroked her hand down Nicole's face. "I remember." Nicole smiled and they looked at each other for a moment. "Come to bed."

She took Jess's hand and walked her over to the hatch. Jess went down the stairs first, and Nicole started down after.

Just before she passed all the way through the hatch, she glanced back at the rocking chair which she could have sworn had moved again.

You, she thought, *are getting sold.*

CHAPTER 4

1955

G race stepped through the door and found herself in a large entryway hall. To the left was a vast reception room; across the way a smaller, more intimate sitting room, and down the hall from the front door the kitchen, opening onto the back garden. In the hall, under the stairs, there was a small wooden door, slightly ajar, and as Grace walked by it she was met with a peculiar smell that seemed to waft up from the basement below. The smell was harsh, bitter; it scratched at her nostrils and coated the back of her throat with the taste of burnt metal and copper pennies. Sister Fitzgerald closed the door and continued to guide her, hand on shoulder, into the large kitchen, where she was told to take a seat at the dark wooden table.

No sooner had she sat down than a man breezed into the room, a long white coat cloaking his body and a cloth mask covering his mouth and nose. *A doctor?*

"You must be Grace," he said, pulling off the mask. He didn't extend his hand to shake but rather stood over her, arms crossed over his chest, and looked her up and down. "Very good," he added, to no one in particular – then spun around, nodded to Sister Fitzgerald and exited the room as suddenly as he'd entered.

Sister Fitzgerald turned to Grace. "Now Grace, you will remain here for the foreseeable, so try to behave and do as you're told."

She never uses my name.

"I must get back to the home, but Dr Baker will be here with you, and some of the other sisters will be calling in from time to time. I'll have Sister Tabitha bring your things this afternoon. Ah, and here is some company for you." Sister Fitzgerald looked to the kitchen door.

Another girl appeared in the doorway, accompanied by a woman Grace took from her uniform to be a nurse. The girl was slightly older than Grace – twenty or twenty-one – with beautiful long blonde hair and eyes so blue they could have been frosted; it was hard to look away from them. The nurse, Grace noticed, was the same one who'd come in to check on Ellen's hand and Grace's own head wound the previous day.

She helped the girl to the opposite end of the table, seating her across from Grace. Then, without a word, she withdrew from the kitchen, leaving Grace alone with the new arrival.

"I'm Grace." Grace kept her voice low, unsure whether anyone was listening outside the door, or if she was even allowed to speak to the girl.

"I'm Isabelle. You can call me Belle," the girl said, with a forced smile. She was beautiful, Grace thought - but weak, too frail for someone her age. "Are you here for treatment too?"

Treatment?

"No, I'm not ill," Grace answered. "I'm not really sure *why* I'm here - maybe to clean? Or keep you company?" She hesitated. "Can I ask what's wrong with *you*?"

"They're not sure. Sometimes I get these fits... and I don't always remember what happens after that. They say it's epilepsy. They say they can make it stop." She sounded unsure. Frightened, even.

"I hope they can." Grace smiled back at her. "How long have you been here?"

"About a week now. They've been monitoring me: how I sleep, how many fits I have, how long they last, things like that. They just took some blood today, but I start the treatment proper tomorrow. They don't tell me too much." She trailed off, gazing blankly not *at* Grace, but *past* her.

Grace, slightly perturbed, stood up from the table to get a better look at the kitchen. "What are we supposed to do now? Can we walk around the house?"

"Yes. We're allowed everywhere except the basement and outside. I mean... we do *go* outside, but not without one of the sisters or a nurse. There are books in the other room." Belle rose, following Grace's lead; it was the most animated Grace had seen her yet. She took Grace by the arm and skipped away, dragging Grace with her out of the kitchen.

G race and Belle spent most of the morning and early afternoon lounging around the big reception room, reading books they'd pulled down from the vast collections lining the walls. They were a mixed bag, the collections: children's books like *Goodnight Moon* side-by-side with *Nineteen Eighty-Four* and other titles Grace had never heard of. And medical books: scientific journals, and dense, strange-looking tomes of psychoanalytic theory.

Sister Tabitha arrived around 1pm with a bag of Grace's things. Grace was relieved to be in the presence of a familiar face. Though seeing her belongings brought home that she had no choice but to stay in the house for the time being, without Ellen.

"Thank you for bringing my things," she told Tabitha. Then: "I wonder, do you know why I'm moving? And for how long? And whether or not I can come back and forth to see the other girls? And—"

"Slow down, Grace. So many questions." Sister Tabitha placed the bag on the ground and raised a hand up to stall the verbal onslaught. "I'm not sure.

All I know is, some of the girls are coming from the home to live here for a few weeks at a time. We have a doctor on site now, so he can help with any medical issues, like Belle's seizures."

"But what about me?" Grace asked, confused. "I don't have fits. What would I want with a doctor?"

"I don't know, Grace. Perhaps they want to monitor you after your dizzy spell, when you banged your head?"

Grace looked awkwardly at the ground: not wanting to contradict whatever story Sister Fitzgerald had made up to justify Grace's placement in the house, but also wondering why she was really there. Then it dawned on her: she was being punished. Punished for lashing out at Sister Fitzgerald, for daring to stand up to her. Which meant it was going to be much harder than before to stay invisible: she'd be on the Sister's radar. Worse, so would Ellen. And if Grace wasn't with her, wasn't living with her, how could she protect her?

The thought of this, of Ellen alone and vulnerable again – it made Grace ache.

Sister Tabitha made supper that night, and the three of them – Tabitha, Grace and Belle – returned to the big wooden table in the kitchen.

Tabitha had on a white shirt open at the collar, her headwear and cape discarded; it made her look, to Grace, like any other 21-year-old. She was more relaxed than she'd been in the main home, too; she even told the girls to call her Tabby, like her mother used to when she was a child. In another life, Grace thought, the three of them could have been friends.

As they were finishing up, Dr Baker appeared in the doorway again, pausing for a moment before he entered. He let out an awkward cough, as if he were about to speak - but didn't. Instead, he walked over to the fridge, brought out a bottle of milk and poured himself a glass of it, wordlessly. The three of them sat in silence.

Grace observed the doctor as he drank. He looked to be in his early forties, his hair dark, brown and short, slicked back with a sort of gel and meticulously kept around his neck – although there were, Grace noticed, flecks of grey developing just above his ears. His eyes were an unusual shade, more grey than blue; he wore tailored pants and shiny black shoes, and his hands looked soft, with perfectly manicured nails. Her father, upon seeing him, would no doubt have remarked that "the man never did a day's work outside in his life."

He awkwardly cleared his throat again, rousing Grace from her evaluation of his character.

"I hope you're all settling into your lodgings?" he said – trying, she thought, but failing to sound relaxed.

She noticed his accent now, though she hadn't previously; he was English, his voice stiff and clipped.

"Everything seems lovely," Sister Tabby answered. "Thank you, Dr Baker".

"Excellent! Very good indeed. Well, I will retire, I think. I'll see you all in the morning." He turned to leave, half-empty glass of milk in hand.

"Doctor?" Grace shot up from the table, anxious to get his attention before he left for the night. "I wonder, can I ask why I'm here? I'm not sick, you see, like Belle." She gestured down at her new friend.

"Well." The doctor shifted awkwardly from one foot to the other, obviously desperate to make his departure. "Sister Fitzgerald volunteered you to come and help us here, with our...projects, and so on."

"What sort of projects?" Grace pressed.

His expression hardened. "You need not concern yourself with the details, child. All is in hand, and you'd do well to remember your place - in this house, and indeed more generally." With that, he made an abrupt exit, an air of hostility hanging in his wake.

"Grace!" Sister Tabitha hissed when he was out of earshot. "You shouldn't be so rude!"

"But I was only asking, is all. I just don't understand—"

"You ought *not* to be asking! Dr Baker and Father Jameson know what they're doing. And you get to live here, in this big new house. You should be grateful for it, so behave yourself."

Sister Tabitha cleared the plates, and together the three of them tidied the kitchen before leaving for their own rooms. The large staircase dominated the hallway. At the top of it was the bathroom, and then round to the left there were four doors leading onto a small single bedroom, a hot-press, and two larger bedrooms, each of which had three beds. The large room at the front had two windows facing out onto the garden; directly across the hall from *that* was the doctor's room, which had its own bathroom.

Grace opted to sleep in the same room as Belle, and Sister Tabby had no objections. The room smelled of fresh paint and the bed, linen, curtains… *everything* looked brand new. Belle went to fetch her toothbrush, then left for the bathroom to ready herself for bed, leaving Grace to explore her new bedroom – feeling its shapes and textures, letting her hand graze over every surface, every unfamiliar material. It was the most privacy she'd had since St. Brigid's had taken her in; since she'd been forced to leave her own home.

From St. Brigid's, her thoughts turned to Ellen – what she might be doing, and whether she knew where Grace had gone. It was a kind of torture, being away from her – not knowing where she was, or when Grace would be allowed to see her again.

She was thinking of Ellen, still, when she spotted something in the corner of the room – by the window, facing out onto the street outside. It was a rocking chair, she saw on closer inspection: painted a brilliant white, a jumping horse carved into its back. She sat down in it; began to rock herself back and forth, gently.

Maybe, she thought, she could find a way to get Ellen here, too. Maybe then they could live together, in this big new house.

Remote though it was, the possibility made her smile, and she settled back into the rocking chair, listening to nothing but the slide of wood across the polished floorboards.

CHAPTER 5

2018

Nicole woke to the sound of birds outside, loud and incessant. The room was already filled with sunlight, and she knew instinctively that she was awake earlier than she wanted to be. She looked across the bed, but it was empty. Glanced at her watch: 7:08am.

Jess is up early.

She headed downstairs; could already hear Jessica inside humming to herself, as she approached the kitchen. Jess was always either singing or humming; she was never quiet, unless she was reading. It was hard to find her sometimes, when she was – tucked away as she tended to be in her own imagination.

"Hey, you're up early." Nicole moved behind Jessica and slipped both arms around her waist. Jess was standing at the sink: looking out over the back garden and sipping on coffee. "Are you tired, after your sleepwalking incident last night?"

"I barely remember it, to be honest." Jess seemed unfazed; unconcerned by what had happened. "Must just be the stress of moving or something."

Nicole walked over to the kettle to make tea.

"Well, as long as you're okay. What are your plans for the day? I'm going to tackle the garden this morning, I think."

"Good for you. I intend, although do not fully commit, to unpack a bit upstairs and set up my new website." She raised both her arms and flexed her muscles, reluctant as ever to take herself even remotely seriously.

Nicole smiled. "You've got this. I have nothing but faith."

The front garden wasn't a huge space. Out to the left of the house was the pebble driveway; the garden lay directly in front, facing out onto the street. Four raised flower beds had been placed charmingly, if haphazardly, around the lawn – not evenly spaced, as Nicole might have expected – and these were her first port of call. She'd need to get a professional in to evaluate the massive willow tree. It looked like it might need to be pruned back a bit, though hopefully not removed entirely.

She set to work on ripping out the weeds. It was another warm day, and she was thankful she'd thought to throw on her denim shorts and a light top. She grabbed weed after leafy green weed in her gardening gloves, twisting and yanking them from the earth. They made a satisfying ripping sound when they relinquished their grip on the soil and came free; it gave her a strange kind of pleasure to hear it, and she found herself lost in the task at hand.

"Hello, hello there, is that yourself Nicole?" Susan's voice bellowed through the black cast iron bars separating the two houses. Nicole jumped, mildly alarmed at the intrusion.

Crap.

It wasn't that Nicole didn't like chatting to people; it was just that she liked to be the one who *chose* when any chats transpired. "Susan! Hi, how are you today? Top of the mornin' to ya, tis a fine day for cutting tur—"

"I'll stop you there love," Susan said. "No-one says that, and you don't have the accent for it. But it is a lovely day." She grinned.

Fair.

"How are you and Jessica getting settled in?" she added.

Nicole walked over to the driveway, closer to where Susan was standing. "All good, thanks. First night went okay – a bit creepy maybe, but you'll have that with a new house, I guess."

"Well, it's a big house, and of course it has that basement. I always found it a bit sinister, if I'm honest. I never liked that wee window at that side facing onto our house." She pointed through the fence at the little glass rectangle that was, Nicole assumed, the window in question. It caught the light peculiarly: the angles and opacity giving it the look, for Nicole, of a portal to another world. It was near ground level and could be easily kicked in by intruders; she made another mental note, this time to get bars put across it for security. Until then, she'd have to make sure they kept the door under the stairs leading down to the basement locked at all times. "Not to mention some of its unfortunate history," Susan continued, whispering slightly. "But I'm sure you came across that when you were researching the house?"

"I did hear a few things about the house," Nicole conceded. "A priest used to live here, right? Back in the day?" She leaned against the bars, sensing Susan had more information to give. She wasn't wrong.

"Oh! I'll come round and tell you all about it, in that case. Hang on there a second." Susan was already making moves out of her own drive.

"Ah. Actually, Susan..."

Nicole panicked; Jess, she was all too aware, would be less than impressed if she arrived back into the house with a guest – and a chatty guest, at that – when Jess was trying to work and the house was still upside-down. "Perhaps I can come round your side? We're not really visitor-ready over here yet."

"Oh, not a bother, love." Susan stopped in her tracks with a crunch of gravel. "Over you come, so – I'll nip in and put the kettle on. We'll sit outside here, 'tis a fine day." She shouted the last bit over her shoulder as she headed inside, presumably to make the promised tea. That was one thing Nicole had noticed about the Irish, in her time in the country: there was no such thing as conversation without tea or coffee. Even if actually drinking it was an optional extra.

What felt like only moments later, Nicole was out in Susan's garden, facing an undeniably impressive spread: scones, two different kinds of jam, whipped cream, and of course the tea, served in a delicate teapot with tiny matching cups and saucers. How, she wondered, had Susan even had time to put together an offering like that? Did she keep it sitting by the front door, on the off-chance someone happened by?

"Now, love, these were freshly baked this morning, so you'll have to try them. The jams are both homemade - the blackcurrant one is from the berries down the back road. Delicious."

Nicole wasn't sure where the back road was, and now she had questions about the hitherto-unknown *front* road it implied, but she wanted to at least try to keep Susan on topic.

"So," she said, diverting the older woman elsewhere, "you were going to give me the lowdown on the house? Bear in mind I already own it. So, you know... be gentle."

She put down her teacup; it clinked as it hit the cast-iron table they were sat at. The whole garden, Nicole noted, was quite the sun-trap – the rays pelting down on them, pleasantly warm on their faces.

Reminds me: I must pick up garden furniture.

Susan seemed serious, suddenly. "Well, they're not the nicest of stories, come to think of it. Maybe you don't need to know. Besides, it's the people that make a home. I'm sure yourself and Jessica will have many happy years in that one." She smiled, albeit weakly, and raised her own tiny cup to her mouth.

Nicole sensed she'd have to press the point a bit - but perhaps not much.

Susan was a storyteller, she suspected. And you didn't break out the scones and two different types of jam just to talk about the weather.

"Come on," she said, returning the smile. "You've got me intrigued now. I promise, I don't scare easy."

Susan hesitated, briefly. "Go on then, so." She leaned in, conspiratorial. "Well, I suppose it all started back in the '50's, when Father Jameson owned the house. It was the parochial house then, so the church owned it. He only lived there."

Susan's voice picked up pace as she spoke: she was, as Nicole had predicted, more than willing to get into the nitty gritty of the house's history. She'd expected Susan to reveal an affair or something similarly illicit: a priest who ran off with a housekeeper, or the like. What unfolded over the next half hour or so, however, was anything but that.

"Do you believe in ghosts yourself, Nicole?" Susan asked – as casually as if she were asking whether Nic took milk in her tea.

Nicole paused midway through buttering a scone, incredulous but faintly amused by the question. "Ghosts?"

Susan *wasn't* amused, and pointedly ignored the sarcasm. "Yes dear - ghosts. Those who have passed away, but who haven't made it to the other side yet. Caught in limbo, if you like."

Jesus Christ.

"I can't say I do, Susan," Nicole said - wondering what she could suddenly remember she had to go and do that would give her an excuse to wrap up the tea party and make her escape. "Are you going to tell me we bought a haunted house?"

"Oh, no! I don't believe in all that—"

"Oh, thank God. For a second there I thought you were completely nu—"

"More of a *cursed* house, I suppose."

"Ah."

Still nuts, then.

"It's just the people that have lived there have been very...unfortunate, you could say." Susan paused for a sip of tea - or for effect, Nicole didn't know.

"Take Father Jameson, for example. He had a sad aul ending."

"What happened to him?" Nicole asked - leaning forward, her voice low. Susan's penchant for the dramatic was infectious, and she felt herself getting caught up in it.

"Well, the house was always owned by the church - I think it was used as offices or something. I know some of the nuns from the home stayed in it, and I think at one point it was a doctor's surgery. Or perhaps the doctor just stayed there, I'm not sure. But I do know by the mid '50's, maybe 1955 or '56, Father Jameson moved in. And that's when things started going wrong."

"Going wrong, how? And what 'home'?" Nicole was all in, now – her scone, forgotten on her plate, claimed by a wasp attracted by the sugar and the colourful jam.

"The girls' home, it was the convent. Then it became an orphanage of sorts. But by the '50's it mainly took in unwed mothers whose families had disowned them."

"God, that's horrible."

"Now Father Jameson, he had a fondness for the bottle. There were rumours about him saying mass drunk and just generally acting the maggot 'round town."

"An alcoholic priest. Okay." Nicole felt mildly relieved at the revelation that the 'cursed house' had in fact only homed a man with a drink problem, and for a short period of time at that. It didn't feel massively disconcerting. "That's not so troubling, surely? Or that uncommon. No offence."

"No offence taken, love. So, you see that big weeping willow tree over at the front of the house?"

Nicole glanced over her shoulder through the iron fence. "Yeah. What about it?"

"That's where they found him hanging. Father Jameson." Susan reached casually for another scone.

"Jesus Christ!" Nicole nearly choked on her tea.

"I know, I shouldn't have another, but they're so much nicer when they're fresh..."

"No, Susan, the priest! He hung himself? On the willow tree? The willow tree in my garden?"

"Oh! Yes dear. Terrible business. I was only a child myself, but it was quite the fuss."

Nicole looked down at her half-eaten scone. The wasp had overstayed its welcome and managed to get itself stuck; the jam, heating up in the sun, had trapped it, holding it in place like slow-moving lava. Nicole took her knife, scooped its dying body out of the molasses and scraped it onto the potted plant by the table.

"Then there were the Bradleys. Now *they* were a lovely couple," Susan said, apparently finding her groove.

"Wait, are they dead?" Nicole held up her hand, unwilling to let Susan bury the lede a second time.

"No love, they're both alive."

"Well, that's something, at least." She picked up the tiny teapot, preparing to pour another mouthful of tea into the tiny cup.

"They did have seven miscarriages in that house, though. Such a shame, it put a terrible strain on them. You know, that house has never had children living in it, not once."

"Oh my god. That's...awful." Nicole set the teapot back down again, no longer sure she should be holding anything too ornate while Susan was telling her story. The older woman had an odd way of speaking; her upbeat tone lured you into a false sense of security. Although Nicole didn't care for maudlin, she felt confident there was probably a happy medium that Susan was not currently striking.

"Poor Mary Bradley took it very hard," Susan went on. "I mean you would, wouldn't you? She had a total breakdown, by all accounts. They had to carry her out of that house with her raving about her babies, it was dreadful. She went into hospital up North somewhere, and do you know? I don't think she ever came out again. But I mean, you'd never be right after that, would you? Poor, poor woman."

Nicole found herself slightly lost for words – but she was the one who wanted the back story, so she persevered. "Okay. So: Father Jameson and the Bradleys. Did anything terrible happen to anyone *else* who lived there?"

"Nooo."

"Susan?"

"Well, I mean no-one who *lived* there. But there was Brian Murphy – he was a gardener, brought in before they tried to sell the house after the priest... you know. Anyway, the church wanted rid of the willow tree, for obvious reasons. And when he was up there with the chainsaw, he lost his footing—"

"Oh, no."

"Yes...lost his footing whilst he was holding the chainsaw, and it was running at the time. It seems he was in a harness, so he didn't fall, but he was sort of...hanging upside down. Anyway, he reaches out to grab a branch as the chainsaw is falling and it catches him right on the shoulder..."

"Jesus."

"...and cuts his whole arm right off. It was rather a mess, I heard. Plus, they didn't find him for a while, so he was sort of, you know... dangling there, bleeding."

Nicole pushed away the bowl of strawberry jam.

"It was the next-door neighbour's dog that sounded the alarm. And by that, I mean he landed into the house covered in blood. He must have rolled around in it, after it had pooled below poor Brian. Then there was Liam McCauley – he was the electrician, brought in to rewire the whole house top to bottom—"

"Did he electrocute himself?"

"Oh no, love - he fell out an open window at the back of the house. Landed awkwardly on the back steps. Broke his neck, died instantly."

"Right." Nicole lifted the back of the iron chair in a pre-emptive bid to stand up, to get away. "Well, this has been lovely, Susan. Thank you." She glanced at the wasp on the leaf. It was already dead.

Of course.

"I don't think they ever did get the house rewired in the end; that wiring must be incredibly old by now. Oh, is that you off, love?" Finally, Susan paused, then stood up herself. "I suppose I've kept you here long enough with all my stories."

"Actually...." Nicole remembered something; something worth checking. "I thought I smelled some burning last night, in the attic. Just for a second, then it was gone."

"That'll be the wiring. You need to get that seen to - that's very dangerous. A little spark up in the attic and suddenly the insulation catches, the inside of the walls are on fire and before you know it, the whole house is in flames."

"Okay - I will, I'll get an electrician in."

"I'll send my Michael round. He's a sparky - I'll get him to come and have a look."

Susan pulled out her mobile phone and fumbled for something Nicole suspected was her glasses. Nicole knew she wore glasses, because those glasses were currently sitting on her head, half obscured by her mop of curls.

"No worries, Susan. I'll get him once we've got the house squared away a bit. You can give him a call then. Thanks again, though - this has been... Thanks."

"Anytime, love. You come over anytime."

Nicole left the garden and hurried back over to her side of the fence – glancing up as she went at the big weeping willow, its catkins gently swaying in the breeze. For a split second, she could've sworn she saw the black robes of a priest's cassock swaying in among them.

She stopped dead and squeezed her eyes shut, willing the image to be washed from her mind.

When she dared to open them again, she saw only the drooping branches.

CHAPTER 6

1955

G race had been in the new house for a full week, and she was bored. She'd been reading a lot, which she loved, but she missed Ellen something awful.

They'd fallen into an easy routine in the house, she and Belle: spending their days together, reading and chatting. Sister Tabitha – Tabby – stayed with them, and would go out with them most afternoons into the garden, where they'd sit in the sun and eat their lunch. Grace still had no idea why *she* was there - but Belle's treatment was due to start after they'd scanned a part of her brain Grace had never heard of.

They'd given Belle medication to stop her from sleeping, in anticipation of the scans; had even brought in an orderly to sit with her at night, to make sure she stayed awake. Belle slept on her own now, in the big room at the front of the house.

The sleep deprivation was telling on her. It was only the little things Grace noticed, at first – things like Belle dropping her cutlery onto her dinner plate or stumbling after a misstep. But it wasn't long before she stopped talking altogether, all her energy consumed by the effort it took her to stay awake. Grace had overheard Tabby asking Dr Baker how long Belle would have to go without sleep, but he'd been vague in his response: it seemed the longer she stayed awake, the more information they thought they'd get when they scanned her brain, though it had sounded to Grace as if the good doctor was speculating, rather than stating facts with any real certainty. Belle was to undergo something called an EEG, and it would map her brain – and hopefully, in doing so, tell the doctor more about her seizures and what brought them about. They thought she might have something called epilepsy, but couldn't yet be certain.

Grace found the clinical aspects of Belle's case fascinating. But she was also growing more and more concerned about Belle herself, and especially the girl's inability to cope with a lack of sleep.

It was on Saturday morning that Father Jameson called over to the house with the newest addition to the household. Jameson – Father Alan Jameson – was the local parish priest, and he was often in the girls' home, where he'd say mass and take confession once a week. He was an odd little man: always smelling of alcohol, and his fingers stained yellow from the tar of his omnipresent cigarettes. Even the front of his blonde hair had yellowed from the train of smoke that was constantly channelling up through it. He was perfectly friendly, one of the few people to talk to Grace like an actual person, but he was always a bit...squirmy, like a man uneasy in his own skin. He was small in stature and had a bit of a belly, as well as a tendency to wear his shirts too small; the black blazer he sported over them strained across his back. His little white dog collar dug tight into his neck, and his face had the red hue of a man under pressure, giving him a look of perpetual discomfort.

One reason for his uneasiness became apparent to Grace not long after she arrived at the girls' home. There were rumours, she'd heard, that the priest had a gambling problem; and, moreover, that some of the monies raised for the church renovation had gone missing on his watch, repurposed by the priest to appease some unsavoury people he'd fallen foul of when he'd been unable to pay out on a bad bet. The rumours eventually died down, and not much more was said about it. Grace hadn't been surprised: priests, even bad ones, were untouchable. They could do no wrong.

"Good morning, girls," the priest said, walking into the main sitting room where Belle and Grace were sitting. Grace was reading, as usual; Belle was nearby, glazed and silent.

"I'd like you to meet Olivia." He gave the girl who'd entered with him a little nudge in the back, and she stepped to the fore.

"Hello," she said, eyes firmly on the ground in front of her.

"It's nice to meet you," said Grace.

Olivia looked up and smiled back at her, though the smile didn't quite make it to her eyes. She looked anxious. Grace noticed her scratching at herself; clearly a habit the new girl had, judging by the deep red grooves on the inside of her left arm. A nervous tic, perhaps – Grace had seen things like it before, in the home. Some of the girls there had scratches or cuts on their arms, always self-inflicted; some pulled at their own hair until it came out in clumps. The nuns normally kept these girls in a separate wing of the home, away from the others. They were often medicated, but never seemed to get better.

"Now, Grace," Father Jameson said, "I want you to look after Olivia while she's staying here. She's to be treated by Dr Baker." His voice dropped slightly. "She suffers from her nerves, so I want you to keep a close eye on her."

"We'll look after her, Father Jameson," Grace agreed. "Come on in, Olivia - I can show you through the books we have." Grace reached out her hand to Olivia, but the new girl didn't take it.

"I want to go home," she said instead.

"Now, now, Olivia," the priest told her. "Enough of that. On you go with Grace and look at the books."

Grace watched as Father Jameson turned on his heel and stepped out into the hallway, where he was greeted by the doctor. The two of them fell into what looked to be deep conversation, and which left her with an uneasy feeling she couldn't shake.

She'd intended to ask the priest about Ellen, but hadn't known what to say. Hadn't known how to phrase the question casually enough to avoid drawing attention.

After a minute or two, the doctor seemed to grow agitated – as if he was arguing with the priest. Grace wanted desperately to hear what they were saying. But as she edged closer to the hallway, the doctor's head snapped up and stared directly at her, leaving her no choice but to smile back at him and close the door.

It was so much harder to be invisible in a house with only five people.

In the afternoon, Sister Tabby reappeared, and the girls went outside to the front lawn. They put blankets on the ground, and Grace sat down on one with a book; Tabby sat near her, and Olivia wandered around the outskirts of the garden. Belle had been brought out in a wheelchair – it was difficult for her to walk now. She'd become even more withdrawn, and was clearly suffering greatly from the sleep deprivation. Grace had overheard the doctor tell Sister Tabby to keep her awake until her scan on Monday.

"It's so beautiful out here. Do you think we should plant some flowers?" Tabby asked Grace, tilting her face to the sun – the only part of her body exposed.

"That might be nice," Grace responded. "I like doing things outside."

"We could have some raised garden beds. Each of you could pick where you wanted to put one and plant your own flowers."

"If they let us, that would be wonderful." Grace, sensing Tabby's relaxed mood, decided to press her for information. "Do you know why Olivia is here? Are they going to treat her?"

Sister Tabby looked around her, seemingly reluctant to entertain Grace's questions. Eventually she answered – but tentatively, and in a lower tone.

"I think so. They say she has schizophrenia. It's a brain disorder: it sometimes makes her see or hear things that aren't there. They say that Doctor Baker has some new treatments from England that might help her. Wouldn't that be great? If he could help Olivia and Belle?"

"Yes, that would be wonderful." Grace let out a sigh, frustrated. "It's just... I still don't know why *I'm* here."

"Oh, I might know something about that. I overheard Sister Fitzgerald chatting to Father Jameson and Doctor Baker. I think you might be here because you're an orphan."

"An orphan? But why would that matter?" Grace was even more confused now.

"I don't know. Maybe they want to study you? You know, to see how it impacted you, being without your parents." Tabby sounded unsure herself, but unconcerned. Though she was five years older than Grace, Tabby seemed to her in some ways more childlike; more innocent than her age suggested.

"They were asking," Tabby continued, "if there were any other orphans, and Sister Fitzgerald mentioned your friend Ellen. So, the good news is: it looks like she'll be coming to stay here from next week."

Grace couldn't believe her ears. Though nothing was clearer, and none of her questions answered, and though something was niggling at her still, deep down, the mention of Ellen changed her mood immediately. She couldn't help but let the smile spread across her face.

Ellen will be here in a few days. Here, with me.

An hour or so passed, and Grace allowed herself to daydream: about Ellen, and how it might be when they were reunited. Then, suddenly, was pulled out of her bliss by a commotion – something in her peripheral vision. Olivia.

The girl was even more agitated than usual: rocking back and forth, and pointing at Belle. Grace and Sister Tabby rose; saw Belle still sitting, as dazed as she'd been for the past couple of days.

As Grace approached, she could see something wasn't right. The right side of Belle's face had started to swell, her cheek ballooning and pushing her eye and mouth up out of their usual position, so that it seemed to Grace as if she were viewing her through the distorting lens of a funhouse mirror. There were raised lumps on Belle's neck; red marks moving up her throat towards her ear.

And a wasp, perched directly below her right eye.

Grace stood for a moment, looking on at her helpless friend. Belle's eyes, she saw, were frantic, panicked, though the rest of her was still, unmoving – as if her body were holding her captive while the wasp stung at her face. A single tear rolled down her cheek.

The wasp, meanwhile, seemed to be resting – steeling itself, perhaps, for another attack. Grace edged nearer, intent on flicking it away... but the wasp moved too, crawling up towards Belle's open, terrified eye. Grace saw a flash of the stinger emerge from the insect's abdomen half a second before it attacked – plunging itself into Belle's glazed eyeball.

Still, Belle didn't move. Was she paralysed, Grace wondered – or just too drugged to defend herself? The wasp's toxins, clearly, were making their way already through her bloodstream, even as it emptied this latest round of venom into her cornea.

"Mother of God, get it off her!" Sister Tabby yelled.

Grace searched for something to scoop the wasp free and away from Belle's eye. She settled on the bookmark, ripping it from between the pages of the book in her hand and using it to leverage the wasp from Belle's cheek. The wasp fell on to the ground, and Grace swiftly threw her book on top of it, killing it, or at the very least immobilising it – then turned immediately back to look at Belle, to try and give her whatever reassurance she could.

It was then Grace heard the *other* buzzing: muffled, obscured. It came not from the dying wasp under the book, but from behind her. From Belle herself.

Grace leaned closer – just as Belle, with much effort, managed to open her mouth ever so slightly. Just enough for Grace to see the *second* wasp inside.

She watched, horrified, as it forced its smooth yellow body from between Belle's lips, manoeuvring left and right as if jostling itself free of a cocoon. Once free, it dropped down into her lap briefly before flying away.

"We need to get her inside," Tabby shouted, sounding every bit as frightened and horrified as Grace felt. "The Doctor needs to look at her, now. At her eye."

"And her mouth." Grace added, barely able to speak.

"What's that?" Tabby said, turning to wheel Belle back inside.

"Make sure he looks inside her mouth too." Guilt prevented Grace from meeting Belle's undamaged eye directly. Instead, she gathered the blankets and turned to pick up her book from the ground.

"Be careful, Grace," Tabby warned her, from over her shoulder. "It'll be angry that you hit it."

Slowly, Grace picked up the book and looked down at the wasp, its slender body now curled in on itself like a sideshow foetus in a jar.

"Don't worry," she said. "It's dead already."

CHAPTER 7

2018

"We need to get rid of the weeping willow tree," Nicole said, bursting through the front door – her raised voice closer to a shout in the echoing void of the house.

"What?" Jessica roared back from somewhere upstairs.

"The willow tree! We need to...where are you?

"Up in the bedroom. We have too much stuff."

Nicole climbed the stairs, two at a time, and hung a left around the top of the banister, down the landing and through the door on the last right. They'd decided on the room at the front of the house for their bedroom: it was big and open, and light poured in through one of the windows, though the other was obscured by the large willow tree outside. The room across from it was equally nice, but slightly smaller; it had its own bathroom, but since neither she nor Jess enjoyed an en suite, they'd early on designated it a guest room, and left it to its own devices.

It was chaos in the bedroom, with boxes open everywhere and an array of creams and sprays dotted about the dresser – but overall, she thought, it looked much more lived in than it had. The homeliness was definitely Jess's doing: Nicole could chitchat with the neighbours and handle the garden, but it was Jess who made a house a home. It always had been.

"What are you roaring about? Is the garden all finished?" Jess glanced out the window, then turned back to Nicole with a raised eyebrow.

"Not exactly. I got one raised bed done, but Susan... called me over for tea." Nicole felt more than slightly sheepish at the admission.

"And how is Susan?"

"She's good. She sends her regards – says she wants you to come round with me next time. Also, the woman can make a scone, and the jam was homemade, really good —"

"Was that what you were shouting up the stairs about? Susan's jam?" Jess was laughing now.

"No, smart ass – I'm getting to that. She was telling me about the house and all the stuff that happened here. And honestly, it's... not great."

"Okay." Jess took a seat on the foot of the bed. "I'm listening."

"Okay. So we knew that a priest used to live here back in the '50's, right? It turns out they found him hanging from that tree right outside our bedroom." Nicole had found herself pacing up and down the bedroom, but stopped at this last revelation to gesture out of the window at the willow tree.

"Hanging how?"

"What do you mean 'hanging how'? From a rope, around his neck."

"Right, sorry. I'm not sure what I was hoping for there." Jessica stood up. "Well, that's unfortunate."

"Susan thinks the house is cursed. Other things happened to other people. She had a list, it was... grim."

Jessica raised her hand. "Wait, cursed? Really? Since when do you believe in that stuff?"

"She was very convincing."

"We're not getting rid of the tree. We both like it and it did nothing wrong, whatever happened to that priest. Babe, horrible things happen all around us all the time: wars fought, lives lost. There's history everywhere." She stood up and walked over to Nicole; draping a comforting arm around her waist. "This is our home. We'll make it a happy one. Okay?"

"Okay." Nicole leaned in to kiss her, but was interrupted by the buzz of her phone in her back pocket. She glanced down at the phone; saw her sister's name lighting up the screen.

Nicole and Louise, her sister, had fallen in love with Ireland together the summer they'd travelled Europe: first with the rugged landscape and friendly locals, then with two very *specific* locals who induced them to stay.

Lou, a psychiatrist, had met Patrick at a talk on mood disorders she'd attended at University College Dublin; they'd married after two years together, and lived now in Dublin with their five-year-old son Ronan. Nicole had met Jessica at a bar in Galway, and after trying and failing to convince her to move to Australia, she'd settled with her in Ireland. They'd lived in Galway City for five years before their wedding; now, two years on, they'd been able finally to move out of the city, to the ocean.

"Is that your sister?" Jess said, letting her arm drop from Nicole's waist. "Are you going to answer?"

"Nah." Nicole shifted uncomfortably where she stood. "I'll call her later."

"Are you avoiding her?"

"No. I'd just rather be with you, you know? I'll call her later. Besides... weren't you going to kiss me?"

"Later," Jess told her, smiling – slipping away from Nicole and out onto the landing.

Later that night, after Jess had brought the bedroom into some sort of order and Nicole had unpacked some kitchen stuff, they headed to bed. Around 3am, Nicole jolted awake, sweating from another nightmare. She'd had a few of them lately; dreams of being trapped, imprisoned, her vision impaired. This time, she'd been stuck in a burning house, the smoke around her dense and choking – unable to see anything, unable find her way out.

"Babe, are you awake?" Nicole reached again, as she had the nights before – but Jess, again, wasn't there.

Nicole stripped back the covers, relieved to feel the rush of cool air on her legs. She stepped out onto the floorboards – determined, yet again, to locate her sleepwalking wife. Once she'd made it out of the bedroom door, she looked automatically upwards – at the hatch above her, leading up to the attic.

Still locked. Thank God.

It was then she heard it: what sounded like running water, the rush of it coming from the opposite end of the landing. She turned her head; noticed the steam seeping out from under the bathroom door.

"Jess? Are you running a bath?"

When no answer came, she began, slowly, to walk along the landing. The sound of the water was thunderous, like a bath overflowing; she quickened her step, and pushed open the door to the bathroom.

Jess stood at the sink, her back to the open door. The room was engulfed in steam, so much that it took Nicole's eyes a second to adjust – reminding her of her dream, of the smoke she'd been lost in. The bath was starting to overflow, and water was spilling out onto the tiles below.

"Jessica!" She was yelling, she realised; practically screaming at Jess's back. "What are you doing?"

The bath tap was running. Nicole reached down to turn it off and found it was red-hot, so hot it burned her hand. She ignored the pain; sunk her wrist into the water to pull out the chain and drain the bath. When she turned around again, Jess was exactly where she'd been before. She hadn't moved, not an inch.

The floor around the sink, however, was shimmering with what looked like broken glass.

Had the bathroom mirror broken? And if it had, why hadn't she heard it shatter?

"Babe, don't move," she told Jessica. "Stay where you are or you'll cut your feet."

She stretched an arm out to her wife, intending to turn her round and guide her away from the broken mirror. At her touch, the woman at the sink turned to face her.

She wasn't Jessica.

Nicole's mouth fell open. The woman in front of her was young, maybe 19 or 20. With the steam beginning to clear, Nicole could see what she was wearing: a long white nightdress embroidered with little pink flowers along the hem. A child's nightdress. Her dark hair was long, but pinned up high on her head – that, Nicole thought, was what had fooled her to begin with, through the steam.

The girl's eyes looked vacant, as if she was looking right through Nicole.

"Who *are* you?" Nicole said.

"My name is Olivia," the girl answered, "and I want to go home."

"What are you doing?" said a voice from behind Nicole.

And there was Jess – the *real* Jess, staring in at the scene from the bathroom doorway.

"What the fuck, Jessica?" Nicole was frantic; confused, and scared out of her mind. "What's going on? What is this?"

She turned back to face Olivia again, just in time to see the girl ram her right hand into the left side of her neck. In that hand, she held a large piece of the broken mirror – and as Nicole watched, began to drag it across her throat from left to right. Her eyes stayed expressionless even as the blood poured down from the ragged, freshly-made slit in her neck, changing the colour of her nightdress from white to pink, from pink to red, and then from red to nearly black with every beat of her heart, every fresh cascade.

Nicole felt the bile rise in her stomach. She couldn't speak; only blink frantically, some unconscious part of her still determined to clear her vision, to sweep away the unreality of the bleeding girl. She felt a pressure on her right arm, and then Jessica was pulling her backwards, out of the bathroom. The last thing she saw before the door slammed shut was Olivia stumbling, falling to her knees on the tiles.

"You're okay," Jess said. "I've got you. I've got you."

She let Jessica wrap her arms around her, but everything felt…off. Wrong, somehow. The landing, too, was hazy, as if there was steam clouding her vision there too. Or smoke, maybe? Her nostrils felt stuffy; again, she smelled talcum powder, the same chalky mineral-vanilla smell she'd picked up in the attic the night before.

Then, as suddenly as the steam had cleared, the sense of *wrongness* receded, and she was back in her body.

"We need to call an ambulance," she said. "Or the guards. *Somebody.*"

"What's wrong?" Jessica said, apparently alarmed herself by Nicole's reaction. Then, softening her voice: "You're okay. Everything is okay."

"What's wrong? What's fucking *wrong*? Are you insane? Did you *see* that?"

Nicole turned back to the door and took another deep breath before opening it wide; steadied herself for a moment, and peered inside.

There was nothing on the bathroom floor but clean white tiles: no mirror, no blood, no water, and no Olivia.

"What the hell?" Nicole whispered, to herself. "You saw that," she added, directing the question this time to her wife. "I know you did."

"Nick, what are you talking about?" Jessica sounded very concerned now – but *just* concerned, Nicole thought. Not frightened. "We should get you back to bed."

"Jessica, you saw that. The girl, the blood."

"Nick, you're scaring me. I didn't *see* anything, and don't know what you're talking about. Come back to bed, okay?"

"Then why did you say that? Why did you say, 'You're okay, I've got you'?"

"Because you were screaming."

"I wasn't screaming." Had *she been screaming, though? She couldn't remember.* "Where were you, anyway? Why weren't you in bed when I woke up?"

"I was downstairs, getting some water." Jessica put a hand on Nicole's arm – gentle, soothing. "Let's go to bed. You must be having a night terror... or, I don't know, *something.*"

"I don't get night terrors, Jess!" Nicole was angry now, the upset and shock replaced by rage and confusion.

"Maybe it's stress related, then. I don't know. But I'm not standing around talking about this anymore. I'm going to bed. Turn off the bathroom light when you're done out here." Jessica walked off towards the bedroom.

"Wait," Nicole called after her, "you said 'what are you doing?' Who were you talking to?"

Jess turned around to face her a final time. "You," she said. "I was talking to *you.* You were standing in the bathroom, screaming at nothing. And now I'm going back to bed. Okay?"

She didn't wait around for Nicole to answer.

CHAPTER 8
1955

T hings took a turn for the worse for Belle, after the wasp stings. Doctor Baker had flushed out her eye and mouth to try to lessen the effects of the poison, but the eye had ballooned up and closed over regardless – so badly that the nurse had to pry it open every day to clean out the pus that oozed from it. Belle's mouth was healing faster than her eye, but not by much.

She'd suffered seventeen wasp stings altogether, including on the inside of her cheek and on her tongue, which had also swollen, to such an extent that she struggled to eat; Sister Tabby had taken to mashing up her food, to make it easier for Belle to swallow. There were also some concerns about her sight: that she might lose it altogether, or that her vision might be permanently impaired.

Doctor Baker still wanted to go ahead with her brain scan, though. When Sister Tabby had complained about Belle's medication, about Belle being unable to move or blink her eyelids, he'd admitted that, yes, the medication affected people differently, and Belle *might* have had too much in her system. But it would all be over soon, he said – because after Belle had the scan, she could sleep for a week if she wanted to.

Grace, meanwhile, was waiting desperately for Ellen to arrive – and Sister Tabby had said that another girl would be coming with her. There'd be five girls in the house then, and Grace was secretly excited at the prospect of having more people around to talk to. Olivia had been terribly upset after the incident in the front garden with Belle, but had calmed down a lot since, and now seemed very attached to the injured girl; Sister Tabby even let Olivia push the wheelchair when Belle had to be moved from the reading room, as they now called it, to the kitchen. Belle's medication had been reduced, though Grace didn't know by how much; she still wasn't allowed to sleep, but was moving more of her own volition, and she seemed more aware of her surroundings.

It had been five days since she'd slept; Dr Baker, Sister Tabby said, would carry out the scan on day seven. That morning, when the nurse had left after cleaning her eye, Grace went in to visit her in the little sitting room across from the reading room – and was relieved to see that Belle turn around to greet her as she entered.

"Well, hello there," Grace said, in as cheery a voice as she could muster. "It's so good to see you moving around a little. I missed you."

Grace tried not to let her revulsion show as she met Belle's face – its skin now pulled and distorted by the masses of swelling and the raised angry red blotches that covered it on one side, from her neck to her hairline. So stretched in places was the skin that it looked to Grace as if it might split open at any moment.

Belle raised her hand, beckoning Grace to sit by her. She tried to speak, but it was clearly painful an effort.

"It's good... to see... you," she mumbled.

Grace put her hand over Belle's. "It's okay, you don't need to speak. I just wanted to come and see you. I can catch you up a bit."

Belle smiled a little, sitting back in her chair while Grace told her all about Ellen and the mystery new girl due to arrive at the house. She told her about Olivia, and how *she* was being treated by Doctor Baker too, for schizophrenia, and that it was Olivia who alerted Grace and Sister Tabby to Belle's condition in the garden. On and on Grace chatted, even confiding in Belle that she thought something odd was going on between the Doctor and Father Jameson; that she'd seen them arguing. Belle listened intently, and it pleased Grace to know her friend was back – if not exactly to her old self, but better at least than she'd been. She was midway through a story about Sister Tabby burning the toast when Belle interrupted her.

"I... can't see," Belle said.

"I know, but it's okay, the nurse said you wouldn't be able to open your eye for a while. It needs to heal, remember."

"But it *is* open." Belle turned to face Grace.

Grace's own eyes widened as she took in Belle's. They looked... well, like the sky, but sky on different days: one the old, brilliant blue that could light up a room, and the other like a grey cloud had passed over it, muting its colour and threatening rain.

"I'll get the doctor," Grace told her. "Don't move. It'll be okay."

Doctor Baker was utterly unmoved, almost robotic as he examined Belle's eye, then offered his findings.

"Well," he said, "there have been cases with corneal stings in which the patient develops cataracts, because of the venom's toxic effect on the anterior lens capsule. Glaucoma and atrophy of the iris can occur, which often leads to some degree of vision loss. The toxic effects of insect venom can also kill eye cells, which can itself lead to temporary, or in some cases permanent partial or complete blindness. Of course, some infections can spread to the other eye as well, but we can hopefully prevent that with antibiotics."

Sister Fitzgerald was called for, and arrived at the house an hour or so later. Grace was still with Belle when she came into the reading room, both of them still very distressed.

"Stop your sniffing, child," the Sister told Belle. "You should be thankful the good Lord forgave enough of your sin to allow you sight in your other eye. We must always look to Christ in our time of despair, mustn't we? 'If your eye causes you to stumble, pluck it out and throw it from you. It is better for you to enter life with one eye, than to have two eyes and be cast into the fiery hell'. Remember, all answers lie in the Good Book, child. If you are ever lost, you will find your way there."

And with that, her homily delivered, she turned and walked right back out of the room.

T he next night, Grace woke to the sound of Belle screaming.

She almost fell out of bed, in her rush to get up and out of the room. Sister Tabby must have done the same, must have heard the screaming too, because when Grace met her on the landing, they met each other's eyes for a moment, then rushed without a word to the other bedroom. It was dark inside; Belle was kneeling on the floor, rocking back and forth, her face in her hands. The orderly tasked with sitting with her through the night and keeping her awake was standing beside her, his hands raised.

"I didn't touch her," he pleaded. "She just started screaming. Then she got down on her knees, and... I think she's praying."

Sister Tabby stepped forward, kneeling down beside Belle in an attempt to soothe her.

"Shush, Belle," she said, rubbing Belle's back, all the while throwing anxious looks over her shoulder to Grace. "It's okay, now – it's me, Sister Tabby, and I've got Grace here too. What's wrong, love? What is it?"

Grace leaned down beside the two of them and stroked Belle's arm. She then reached up to move Belle's hand that were currently covering her eyes as she rocked back and forth in the darkness and mumbled Hail Marys. It was then Grace felt it: the wet, sticky substance on her fingers.

Belle turned her head to Grace, and opened both of her eyelids – revealing the pulpish, cavernous voids where her eyes should have been, the blood running down her cheeks.

"'I will lead the blind by ways they have not known,'" she said. "'Along unfamiliar paths I will guide them; I will turn the darkness into light before them and make the rough places smooth. These are the things I will do; I will not forsake them.'"

The force of the words, softly spoken though they were, repelled Grace, and she stumbled backwards before getting shakily to her feet. She glanced down at her own hands and saw, by the light of the moon through the window, that they were bathed in what could only be Belle's blood.

"Oh Belle, what have you done?" she said, to herself as much as to Sister Tabby.

Tabby turned on the light, revealing the true horror of the tableau. Tabby screamed, the sound reverberating around the room; brought her own hands to her face, and screamed again on realising they, too, were bloody.

Belle stayed on her knees, eyes wide open – sightless, useless.

Grace surveyed the scene before her: Belle, kneeling in a pool of her own blood, her blond hair matted and darkened by so much gore that it stuck to her face, framing open eyelids that revealed the absence of her kind blue eyes. The void left behind was foreign and strange, the ragged red flesh ripped, as if a stone had been pulled from a peach. Grace felt her stomach heave.

Just in front of Belle's right knee, something caught the light: a small object, glinting.

A teaspoon. A silver teaspoon, dripping with blood.

Still, Sister Tabby screamed.

"Tabitha! Please!" Grace shouted – in a tone, she'd recall later, that would have been unthinkable even minutes before.

The reprimand shocked Tabby into silence. Seconds later, Doctor Baker ran into the room, wrapping his dark navy dressing gown around his body – and looking, Grace thought, remarkably suave, even at 3am. Even in the midst of a bloodbath.

"What's happening in here?" he asked Tabby.

Belle had her back to him; Grace was twelve feet away, on the other side of the room. It was clear, however, that Tabby was in no position to provide him with answers.

It was up to Grace to tell him; only Grace.

"Her eyeballs," she said," surprised how calm she seemed, how unperturbed. "She scooped them out with a teaspoon."

He stared back at Grace, astonished – then, stepping forward, saw the blood.

Belle, still kneeling, rotated her head to look at him. His mouth opened slowly, then shut as he took her in.

"What have you done, girl?" he said.

Grace found the lack of panic in his tone more disturbing than comforting. It wasn't just calm professionalism, she thought; more likely a complete lack of concern for Belle's wellbeing, or a morbid, voyeuristic curiosity.

"Sister Tabby," he said, "go at once and get my medical bag. Then, when you've brought it, go and call Father Jameson. Tell him..." The Doctor glanced down at Belle, at the eyeballs – still dangling from their optic nerves – she held cupped in her hands like unravelled yoyos. "Tell him...there's been an incident."

The orderly was let go, Grace discovered the next morning, on entering the kitchen and overhearing Doctor Baker argue with Sister Tabby – rather ironically, for falling asleep at his post.

74

Then:

"It's barbaric," Tabby said, speaking now of Belle and not the orderly. "She's been through enough. She's clearly lost her mind." The young nun looked exhausted, Grace thought – but riled up, nevertheless.

The Doctor, by contrast, sounded almost excited beneath his irritation at being questioned by a woman. "She will have the scan – there's no point in turning back now. Besides, this is the perfect time to map the brain, after a psychotic episode. *Imagine* what we might discover."

"But...," Tabby persisted.

"Enough! I will not be questioned further on this by... *you*. These are my trials, and my decision is final. Get her ready to leave. You have one hour."

Exactly an hour later, Belle left the house to have her scan. Her eyes were bandaged, but she was awake. Grace grabbed her hand as she was wheeled out the front door, leaning down until she was level with Belle's ear.

"I'm sorry," she whispered, guilt making her hoarse. "I'm so sorry."

In five hours, Belle was home again. Doctor Baker granted her permission to she go straight up to her room – now, he said, she could sleep as long as she wanted, and would not be disturbed.

For Grace, there was relief: that it was finally over, and her friend could rest at last.

What she didn't know, however – and what only Doctor Baker and the nurse might have suspected – was that, after a prolonged period of sleep deprivation, the brain is more susceptible to seizures. And so it came to be that, at 4am the next morning, Belle's already broken body, now blind and eyeless, began to twitch and stiffen. Her limbs shook violently and she struggled to catch her breath – and she fell, finally, into an unconsciousness from which she'd never wake.

G race watched the undertaker pull the white sheet over Belle's face – though not before she registered that, yes, they'd stitched her eyes shut.

The Doctor, she'd begun to realise, was just experimenting with them: guessing at treatments and playing out his own half-baked theories, and with impunity, because no-one cared. Because they were nothing, she and the other girls in the house; they were expendable.

She leaned back against the wall in the hallway, the full weight of that realisation hit. Tears welled in her eyes, a sense of hopelessness washing over her.

She forced her eyelids shut and turned her head to the left, away from Belle and the undertaker as he wheeled her away through the rear of the house – releasing them again just in time to catch sight of a car, a black saloon, as it pulled up into the drive at the front of the house.

The door of the car opened, and out stepped Ellen – who, seeing Grace in the doorway of Montpellier Street, beamed with the unbridled joy of someone who'd finally come home.

CHAPTER 9

2018

Nicole was one hundred percent sure of what she'd seen: a girl, slashing her own throat in the bathroom of her and Jessica's new home before disappearing into thin air.

The immediate aftermath had been tense. Jess had gone back to bed and slept through the night, but Nicole had lain awake, her eyes open, the scene from the bathroom replaying over and over in her mind. She could see the girl so clearly; could feel the steam from the hot water on her skin, that damp, clammy heat. It had felt...real. So very real.

Three days on, and she and Jess still hadn't really talked about it, though nothing else strange had happened since. They'd been working around the house for the most part, organising the kitchen and picking out new paint colours for the walls. The new bookcase had been delivered; Nicole was putting it together in the main hallway, in fact, when the knock at the front door came.

She rose from her crouching position at the sound, dusting off her jeans and accidently kicking a little pile of neatly separated screws in the process. The screws scattered across the floor, reminding her of the kind of cockroaches that scurried away in all directions when you turned on a light in a hostel room at 4am.

Fuck.

She made her way over to the door and opened it, revealing a smiling Susan on the doorstep.

"Howareya, love? I brought over some scones." The old woman held the proffered bake goods aloft on a little plate, a tea towel draped over them. "I hadn't seen you out and about much, so I told my Billy I'd pop round and see how you're getting on."

Not waiting for a response, Susan brushed past Nicole, into the hallway.

"Well, come on in," Nicole said, already closing the door behind her. "Sorry about the mess, it's been a slow process."

"I'd put all those screws in one pile, dear; easier to see what you're doing when they're not spread all across the hall like that." She made a beeline for the kitchen, Nicole at her heels. "God, I haven't been in this house in years."

"Yes, I...never mind, just go through, I'll be right there." Nicole considered pushing the scattered screws into a single pile with her shoe, for the sake of appearances, then gave up and followed Susan into the kitchen – where Susan was standing, her mouth ajar and her face frozen in horror.

"I know," Nicole told her, glancing around at the clutter, "it's a bit of a mess still."

"A bit of a mess?" Susan sounded shocked. "Jaysus, you'd need a *team* of people to sort this place out."

"Yeah, we need to get on it. Anyway: how are you, Susan? Cup of tea?"

"Go on then, love, why not? I'll sort the scones out here at the table." The older woman lifted a box out of the way and placed it carefully on the ground. "So, how are things going?" she asked, while Nicole put the kettle on to boil. "I hope you don't mind me saying, but you look a bit...knackered." She treated Nicole to a quick but emphatic once-over.

"Yeah, it's just been a lot, trying to sort the house while Jess sets up a business. She's a web designer, so she's trying to launch that and it's..." She trailed off, momentarily lost for words. "It's a lot."

"And things with the house?" Susan's tone was suspiciously casual. As she spoke, she pulled out the chair beside her, prompting Nicole to join her at the table, and bring the tea.

"The house? Yeah, everything's fine." She didn't meet Susan's eye, irrationally afraid the woman would somehow be able to read her mind. There was something about the way she looked at you, with that curly head slightly tilted to the side, that suggest both a capacity for insight and an unshakeable tenacity – as if she were trying to work out the image hidden in a Magic Eye picture, and wouldn't rest until she'd puzzled it out. "Well, okay," she admitted after a beat, still avoiding Susan's interrogatory gaze, "it *has* been a little bit peculiar. Our sleeping has been really messed up. I've been having strange, really vivid nightmares, and Jess has been sleepwalking. She used to do it, before we moved here – sleepwalk, I mean. But not for years. The house just seems to be having... a weird effect on us."

Finally, she looked up. Susan it appeared, had been in the process of cutting a scone while Nicole had been speaking – but had stopped mid-way, leaving the scone dramatically suspended in the air, as if both she and it had been frozen in time.

"What?" Nicole said.

"You've both been awake in the night?"

"Well, yeah, a bit. We assumed it was the move, the stress of it."

"Could be, could be. But this house has the habit of unsettling people. I was hoping it would...let you be." Susan took a pensive sip of her tea.

"Let us be?" Nicole scoffed slightly. "What exactly do you think it does to people? It's just a house: walls and door and a roof."

Susan lowered her cup. "It's not the house love, it's what the house has seen. What happened *under* the roof, *between* the walls."

"Look, Susan, I don't want to be rude, and you really have been so lovely, but I don't need any superstition right now. I get that unfortunate things have happened here, that people have been hurt and died. But like Jess said when I told her, that's true of anywhere. History's all around us."

She was trying to stay calm, but her tone was harsher than she'd have liked. She didn't want to offend her new neighbour – the closest thing she had to a friend in these parts.

Susan seemed to consider this for a moment. "Yes, Jessica has a point, I suppose, but tell me—what happened in this nightmare?"

"I don't know. It was just, like... one of those *creepy person in the house* type nightmares, you know?"

Nicole had zero desire to discuss it. In fact, she'd actively tried to avoid even thinking about it since that night.

"Where were they, the person? What did they look like? Did they speak? What did they say? What were they wearing?"

"Alright, Susan! Stop with the questions, I'll just tell you about it, okay?" Nicole put her knife down. "So, I woke up a few nights ago—well, I *think* I woke up, I guess I didn't really, I mean not technically, because it was a dream..."

Susan sighed and made a *get on with it* gesture with one hand.

"Right. Fine. So, I get up... and Jess isn't in the room."

She began to recount the events of the night—the girl in the bathroom, Jess not seeing her. "The girl – she slit her throat with a big shard of the mirror," she said. "She was looking right at me. She just pulled it across her throat. Didn't cry out or anything." Nicole's voice waivered slightly as she recalled the image. She could hear it: the sound, the...the tearing.

Then, quite unexpectedly, she was crying. She could see the blood now, clear as day, flowing from the gash in the girl's throat; the piece of ragged skin hanging down and her eyes unblinking as she stared dead ahead. Her life draining away while Nicole looked on.

"It sounds like you had quite the shock," Susan said – seeming unconcerned as she stirred sugar into her tea and clinked the teaspoon on top of the little cup.

Nicole sniffled and straightened her back, suddenly self-conscious of her show of emotion.

"Well, yes, actually it was extremely upsetting, Susan," she said, wiping her eyes.

"Oh, I know, dear, I know. It's very upsetting meeting Olivia for the first time."

Nicole's head shot up. "What did you just say?"

"Olivia— the girl in the bathroom? The first impression she leaves is always...extreme. But wait until you meet Belle." Susan exhaled loudly. "She'll make your eyes pop out."

CHAPTER 10

1955

Ellen smiled at Grace, and started up the front steps, into the house. She was accompanied by two other girls – and a nun, one whom Grace didn't recognise but assumed would be staying at the very least overnight in Montpellier Street, since Sister Tabby was taking a few days leave to settle her nerves.

No-one, Grace had noticed when she'd heard Tabby's news, seemed to care much about *her*, or how the final days of Belle's life might have affected her.

It was a relief to see Ellen, an enormous relief – but Grace found she was scared, too. Scared of what Ellen might be walking into, what might lie ahead of her in the Doctor's house; what other experiments he might see fit to perform.

What if I can't protect her?

"You must be Grace," the nun said.

Grace put out her hand. "It's nice to meet you."

"I'm Sister Angela, and this is Ellen, Ruth and Sinead." The old nun gestured behind her at the three girls lined up by the front door, though Grace's eyes stayed firmly on Ellen. "Is Doctor Baker here?"

"I think he's through in the kitchen." Grace pointed over her shoulder.

"Very well, I'll tell him we're here. And Grace, you might show the girls upstairs so they can put their bags away."

Sister Angela shuffled off into the house, leaving the girls to their own devices.

"It's so good to see you," Ellen said, pulling Grace into a hug.

Grace let herself relax for a moment, before the reality of her current situation intruded in, the dark reclaiming the brief burst of light Ellen had brought.

"Are you okay?" Ellen asked, feeling Grace stiffen in her arms.

"Let's go upstairs," Grace said quietly. "We can talk there." She turned to face Ruth and Sinead, finally taking them in, and added, a little louder: "Follow me and I'll show you to the bedrooms."

Ruth was older than the other girls; 27 or 28, Grace thought, and friendly-looking, her smile wide and open, deep dimples in her cheeks. Blonde, shoulder-length hair framed her face.

She was also heavily pregnant – a protective hand shielding the large bump at her stomach as she followed Grace into the house and up the stairs to the bedrooms.

Sinead seemed more demure, on first glance; more subdued, her head hanging low and her blue eyes never quite meeting Grace's. She had curly hair and a slightly crooked front tooth, and she walked as if she carried the weight of the world on her shoulders.

As soon as they reached the first floor, Ruth sought out a toilet.

"Sorry," she said, stroking her belly and making as much of a dash as she could muster into the bathroom at the top of the stairs. "This little fella likes to sit right on my bladder."

Grace ushered Sinead and Ellen into the first bedroom, where Olivia and Grace herself slept. There was only one empty bed now; and Grace, she realised as she showed the inside, very much wanted Ellen to be the one sleeping in it. Her heart sank, then, when Sinead wandered over to the bed and put her case on top of it, before sitting silently down beside it and seeming to lose herself in thought.

"I guess that'll be Sinead's bed, then," Ellen whispered.

"I guess so," Grace said, not quite able to keep the disappointment from her voice.

Ellen brushed her hand against Grace's, just for a second, and smiled. "Come on, then – show me my room."

Grace smiled back; how could she be anything but content in Ellen's company, no matter where they slept? "Okay, then – follow me."

"I'm going next door with Grace to see my room, okay?" Ellen told Sinead. When no response was forthcoming, they made their exit.

Out on the landing, Grace turned to Ellen. "So, what's up with her?"

"Ah. Well, Sinead already had her baby, about two weeks ago, but it was taken away. She really hasn't spoken much since."

"Oh my God, that's awful. Taken away where?" Grace continued along the landing and took the right into the other room.

"Well, no-one really knows," Ellen said, following her. "But there was rumour that the nuns had her sign some papers before she went into labour, and that the baby was given to a couple somewhere in Cork."

Grace paused at the door to the second bedroom. "How can they do that, just take someone's child and give it away? It's horrible, so horrible."

Ellen put a hand on Grace's arm. "I know, but the baby's gone. Sinead didn't even get a chance to say goodbye. She hasn't told anyone what happened, either. Hasn't said much of anything since."

Grace should have been enraged, she knew – but couldn't help but be distracted by Ellen's hand on her arm. It was warm and calming, Grace's shoulders relaxing and her breathing steadying in response to the touch.

"So, then," Ellen said, still smiling. "This is my room?"

Grace looked around. The last time she'd been in the room, Belle had been drenched in blood and screaming – right after scooping out her own eyes. The memory alone made her shiver.

"Are you okay?" Ellen asked.

"Yeah, I'm fine. And yes – this is your new room." Grace swallowed her disquiet and marched into the centre of the room, her hands spread wide. "Welcome home," she said with a smile.

"Why thank you." Ellen threw her case up onto the first bed – what had been Belle's bed.

"Not that one," Grace said automatically, lifting the case and moving it onto the second bed without explanation.

Ellen didn't question her decision. Instead, she walked over to Grace and gave her another hug – her body soft but solid against Grace's. "I missed you."

They were holding each other, still, when Ruth made her presence known from the doorway, clearing her throat to alert the younger girls to her arrival. Grace had no sense of how long Ruth had been watching them.

"Sorry to interrupt," she said, with a smile of her own. "But I wasn't going to get much out of Chatty Cathy next door. Are there just the two rooms?"

"Yes," Grace confirmed. "The three beds in here are free, and there *was* one next door with me and Olivia, but it looks like Sinead might have claimed it."

Ruth stood stock-still for an instant, still studying them both.

"Well," she said after a moment, "I hate to complicate matters, but I think I'm going to need you to swap rooms with me." She stared pointedly at Grace.

"You are?" Grace asked her.

"Yes. I'm sorry, but I have to pee roughly a hundred times a night, and I *need* to be near the bathroom. I hope you don't mind."

Her smile widened – suggesting, Grace thought, that she knew neither Grace nor Ellen would mind at all.

A little while later, with the beds made and the rooms swapped, Grace, Ellen and Ruth allowed themselves a rest and a catch-up. Sinead was napping in the other room, and Sister Angela was still downstairs with Doctor Baker – and now Father Jameson, whose car had pulled up outside twenty minutes earlier, and whose whiskey-soaked voice now echoed, unmodulated, along the hallway.

The last hour or so had been a welcome distraction for Grace. She laughed as Ruth regaled them with stories from her childhood, of growing up on a farm in the Midlands with a pack of five brothers, all younger than her; it sounded as if not a day had passed there free of some sort of calamity or near-death experience, a jumping off a barn roof and or a misjudging of a landing. Ruth laughed so hard she cried, recounting them. The mood was light, happy even – but as soon had Grace allowed herself to acknowledge it, a familiar dread overcame her, sinking into her bones and weighing her down.

"So, did they tell you why you were being moved here?" Grace asked, doing her best to sound casual.

It was a relief to have Ruth and Ellen there with her; maybe together they could do something, help each other. Olivia and Sinead, she suspected, had their own issues, just as Belle had; they couldn't see what was happening around them, blinded as they were by a fog of medication and deafened by the voices in their heads.

"Well, a little bit," Ruth said. "Apparently the doctor has some new vaccine for pregnant women. It's supposed to help the baby stay fit and strong." She looked down at her stomach and stroked it, lovingly.

"I have no idea why I'm here," Ellen said. "Sister Fitzgerald just told me to pack my things; I wasn't even sure where I was going. It was Sister Tabby who told me it was just around the corner. And that you were here," she added, smiling at Grace.

Grace smiled back at Ellen, and Ruth seemed to study both of them again before continuing.

"I think it's pretty clear why Sinead is here," she said.

"Is that really true?" Grace was still struggling to believe what Ellen had told her about Sinead, the utter horror of it. "Ellen said they took away her baby, and she hasn't spoken since."

Ruth nodded. "Pretty much. A few days before the birth she was given bed rest, and on one of the days a new doctor came in, an English man. Doctor...Barber, maybe?"

"Doctor Baker?" said Grace.

"Baker! Yes, that's it. Ugh, my brain these days. So, he comes in, this Doctor Baker, and gets her to sign some papers. Father Jameson was there too, and I think Sister Fitz, so I assumed it was all above board. But it seems they were adoption papers, and the baby was removed straight after Sinead gave birth. They wouldn't even let her see it. Said it would be 'too difficult' for her."

"Doctor Baker is in charge of this house." Grace thought it best to get to the point. "And to be honest, I don't think we should be trusting him. Him *or* Father Jameson."

Grace paused to gauge the reaction in the room. Ellen looked shocked, and Ruth, she saw, looked outright scared; she had both hands on her pregnant belly now, and however vulnerable Grace felt, she realised Ruth must had felt the same, but tenfold.

"We really need to stick together," she said. "What he did to Belle... it wasn't right. We need to find out what's going on here. What he's up to, the Doctor, and how – why – Father Jameson would be helping him."

The other girls nodded their agreement.

"Oh, *here* you all are!" Sister Angela appeared at the bedroom door, Sinead hovering at her shoulder. "Time to come downstairs, girls – we need to get the dinner started. I was just speaking with Doctor Baker. And what a charming gentleman he is!"

CHAPTER 11
2018

"How did you know her name?" Nicole was standing up now, but Susan hadn't moved; she was still sipping her tea.

"Do sit down, love. I can't be staring up at you, not with my bad neck."

Begrudgingly, Nicole lowered herself back into her seat.

"I hope you don't mind me saying, dear," Susan continued, "but you have a bit of a flair for the dramatic."

"Me? *I'm* dramatic? You just *named* the ghost in my house. I've been over here trying to figure out if I'm going mad, and you already know all about her."

"Them."

"What's that, now?"

"It's *them*, not *she*. There's more than one of them, dear." Susan topped up her tea.

"Right, of course." Nicole tried to stay calm. "*How* many, then?"

"I couldn't say for sure. I mean, there are at least three that I know of, all girls. I tried to look into it, years back, to see if I could track them down. I was expecting a *Family Of five In House Fire, three Sisters Killed* type headline, but there was nothing. The church owned the house some time back, I think I told you that already. But there are no records of any deaths at the property from that time period – not one. It's all very odd."

"We can't tell Jessica about this – not yet. Not until we know more. She's stressed enough already, she doesn't need more on her plate."

"Well, I haven't met her yet," Susan said, sounding faintly offended, "but it wasn't the first thing I was planning to announce, when I finally do."

"About that." Nicole felt her own tone change, low-key panic supplanted by mild irritation. "I was at your house. We talked about people dying here, and you didn't think to maybe give me a heads-up *then* about the trio?"

"I'm not sure they sing, dear."

"You know exactly what I mean, Susan."

"Well, I mean… not everyone can see them, so it didn't seem necessary to mention them right from the off. What if you *never* saw them, and I'd been banging on about the ghosts of three girls haunting your house? Sure, you'd think I was mad in the head. We'd never get you round for our New Year's Eve do then."

"How often do you think it'll happen?" If she was going to be living with ghosts, Nicole figured, she wanted to gather as much information on them as possible. Forewarned was forearmed, wasn't it?

"Well, we just do it the once, love…on New Year's Eve. Is it different in Australia?"

"The ghosts, Susan. How often do the ghosts come visiting?"

"Oh! Oh, I see. I'm not really sure. But they're here in the house the whole time, as I understand it. Have been for decades."

"This is a nightmare." Nicole felt her panic rising again, her palms beginning to sweat. It couldn't be real, could it? None of this could be real. "I mean, obviously you worry, don't you, when you buy a house? You wonder what the neighbours'll be like, whether there'll be a dog next door that won't stop won't barking. Things like that. But ghosts? *Three* ghosts in your bloody bathroom?" She put her head in her hands.

"Have you done any stage work, dear?"

"This isn't me being dramatic, Susan! There are actual ghosts, in my house." She paused; tried to get a grip on herself. "What do they want? That one who cut her own throat – why couldn't Jessica see her?"

"Ah, well, that's what I was saying, you see. Not everyone *can* see them – just people who are... open to it. That's why I didn't mention it before. But even those who can't see them can be affected by them. They can start... acting strangely, if you know what I mean. So you might want to watch out for Jessica. Keep an extra eye on her."

"Oh, God. Do you think they could hurt her?"

"Well, they're dead, love, aren't they? So I'd say you have the upper hand there." Susan glanced around the kitchen. "Are you sure you wouldn't want a hand yourself, sorting out the place a bit?"

"I told you, it's fine, I can..."

A loud bang from upstairs interrupted her, mid-sentence.

"That must be Jess," she said, nervously, throwing a look at the ceiling. "She's moving things around up there."

"Oh, I didn't hear anything, dear," Susan told her. "First your eyes go," she pointed to her glasses, "then your ears." She turned her head, giving Nicole a glimpse of the hearing aid nestling in her left ear. "That's all ahead of you, of course."

Strangely, Nicole found herself relaxing a little. Susan, despite her idiosyncrasies, had a calming way about her. She was unflustered, and Nicole felt oddly comforted by her presence. She reminded Nic of her mother, despite being at least ten years younger.

"So how do you know about the ghosts?" she asked. "Have *you* seen them?"

"Well, there were rumours, from time to time. I thought they were old wives's tales, to be quite honest; I wouldn't believe in that type of thing, normally. But then strange things started happening to the people living in

the house. They'd be kept up all night by noises and one thing or another...
and lack of sleep can really have an effect on people, you know? Then one day
I was out in my back garden, and I saw a girl myself, through the window, just
staring out. And when I waved, she didn't move – just... stood there, looking
through me, fidgeting with something around her neck. A chain, I think it was."

"But that could have been anyone," Nicole said. "Just someone in the
house. I mean, how did you know she was a ghost? Did she look, you know...
dead?"

"No, she didn't *look* dead! But the house was vacant then, and there was
definitely no one living there...and there she was anyway, in that window,
staring down at me. She was young—seventeen, eighteen maybe. Mad curly
hair she had, too – bigger than mine, even." Susan smiled at the memory. "I
haven't seen her in a while. But I swear on my life she was there."

Nicole shifted in her seat. "Okay. So we've got the girl with the curly hair
at the window, and the girl I saw in the bathroom – what did you say her
name was, Olivia? And that other one you mentioned – Belle?"

"Ah, yes, Belle. She tends to be seen in the larger upstairs bedroom at the
front of the house—"

Nicole's heart sank. "That's our bedroom. Jess is up there right now."

"Well, she's fairly harmless."

"Fairly?"

"It's more her appearance that can be disconcerting, I suppose. She can
shock people, and if you were, for instance, up a ladder or at the top of the
stairs, the way she looks might, you know... distract you."

Nicole raised an eyebrow. "What does she look like?"

"I haven't actually *met* Belle, you understand. But apparently her eyes are
sort of...Well, they're just...She doesn't *have* any, is the thing."

"Oh my God." Nicole put her hand over her mouth. "*Oh my god.*"

"What's wrong, dear?" Susan wrapped her hand around Nicole's. It was
cold, and the feel of it snapped Nicole back to the moment.

"The other night, when I woke up and Jess was in the attic, she was sleepwalking – but when I got to her, she turned around and for a second — just a split second — her eyes looked strange. I thought they were black, but I think maybe they were... missing? It was late, and it was dark, and I thought I was seeing things, but...*fuck*."

"Language, dear." Susan tilted her head in disapproval. "I know it's a lot to take in, but there's really no need to be so uncouth."

"Sorry," Nicole muttered, suitably chastised.

"There really is nothing to worry about, love. Why don't you get Jessica down here? I can meet her, and we can all talk together about the girls, have a nice cup of tea and a chat. She can try one of my scones, too. It'll be grand."

"Maybe I should speak to Jess first, before you do. She's a bit sensitive lately. Her father passed away four months ago and it hit her hard – they were awfully close."

"Interesting..."

"What? What's interesting?"

Nicole's phone rang, the vibrations amplifying as they travelled along the table.

"Do you need to get that, dear?" Susan said. "Don't mind me, if you do."

Nicole picked it up and glanced at the caller ID before rejecting the call and returning the phone to the table, face-down. "No, it's fine. It's just my sister – I can call her back. I'm sorry, what were you saying?"

"Well," Susan continued, "they say that those who have encountered death recently are more, you know... *susceptible* to the spirit world. To seeing it; feeling its presence and the like."

"But Jess *didn't* see the girl. She hasn't seen or felt anything, at least not that she's told me."

Susan pondered this for a moment. "It's only a theory, I suppose. But you said she was walking around at night and up in the attic, that her eyes looked…different? It could be they're affecting her too, the ghosts, but she's just not aware of it yet. We really should talk to her."

She sounded more serious now, Nicole thought; had departed from her usual easy-going manner. There was a certain urgency in her tone, too; a concern that hadn't been there previously.

"I'm going to start researching again," Nicole said. "See what I can find out. There's far more information out there now, more ways of getting to it. Would you like to help?"

Susan didn't hesitate. "Absolutely, love. I'll bring over those notes I gathered from before, years back."

"Brilliant. Maybe if we can find out who they are and what happened to them, we can find out why they're still here. Find out how we can help them leave."

"Help who leave?"

For the second time that day, Nicole started in her seat. She looked up, and there was Jessica, standing at the kitchen door.

"God," she said, "you scared me."

"Sorry, dear?" Susan was still looking at Nicole; fiddling now with her hearing aid.

"Oh, sorry, Susan. This is my wife, Jessica." Nicole pointed Jess's way.

Susan turned in her chair, to face the doorway behind her.

"And this is the wonderful Susan I've been telling you about," Nicole told her wife. "Do you want a cup of tea?"

"Hi, Susan," Jess said, smiling. "I've heard a lot about you. And go on, then. I need a break from that bloody computer."

Nicole took another teacup down from the shelf; filled it to the brim, and sat back down across from Susan.

"Susan's been telling me some interesting stuff about the house," she said.

"So I have," Susan agreed, glancing up at Jess and then back at Nicole. "And I have a feeling things are about to get a lot more interesting, at that."

CHAPTER 12
1955

A week on from Ellen's arrival, and Olivia was deep into her treatment. She'd respond well, Dr Baker had said, to electroconvulsive therapy – and whilst Grace wasn't altogether sure what that involved, she thought it sounded like torture. From the scraps of conversation between the nuns, the Doctor and Father Jameson they'd overheard, the girls had pieced together what the men believed was actually wrong with Olivia. She was schizophrenic, or so the Doctor believed. But sending shockwaves through certain parts of her brain could treat the symptoms, and thereby eradicate the condition.

"Shockwaves?" said Ruth. She was washing up the breakfast dishes by the sink while Grace dried. "How does that work?"

"Well, I don't know." Grace took another plate from Ruth. "It must be electric, mustn't it?"

"Do you think it hurts?" Ruth winced in sympathy at the prospect.

"I hope not. They'll put her under some sort of anaesthetic, won't they? In that room downstairs."

Downstairs meant the basement. Dr Baker spent a lot of time there, but none of the girls had ever seen it, ever been inside; only caught the lingering traces of the harsh chemicals that wafted up on occasion into the rest of the house. Grace had been waiting for an opportunity to get a proper look around: seeing where he worked, she hoped, would shed some light on who Dr Baker really was, on what his plans might be, and on whether or not she and her friends might be subjected to any other of his 'treatments'.

"You know, I just thought of something," she said. "There are medical journals on the bookshelf in the sitting room. I could go and look them up, see if I can find anything on this electroshock treatment. You could come join me, when we've finished up here."

And, in fact, the sitting room bookshelf proved very helpful indeed. Grace scanned the spines of the medical texts organised along the lower shelves until she reached one titled, promisingly, A Handbook of Clinical Psychiatry. She slid it free of the others; opened it, and went straight to the index.

And there it was: an entry on Electroconvulsive Therapy.

Electroconvulsive therapy, she read, *is a treatment that involves sending an electric current through the brain, causing a brief surge of electrical activity within the patient's brain (also known as a seizure). The aim of the treatment is to relieve the symptoms of some mental health problems.*

Causing seizures? *Jesus Christ.*

A shadow fell across the pages of the book – someone entering the room. Ruth?

"You're not going to believe this," she said, without looking up. "He's going to electrocute her brain until she has a seizure..."

"Well, that's a crude assessment. But essentially, yes."

"Dr Baker." Grace stood up and slammed the journal shut, panic flooding her system. "I was just reading, I'm so sorry if I disturbed your things."

"You have such a curious mind, Grace. Always seeking out answers, sometimes to questions you shouldn't be asking. Tell me: what would you like to know about electroconvulsive therapy?"

He was calm, unusually so; it was unsettling, uncomfortable, not least because she suspected a fit of anger would soon follow. His mood swings were legendary in the house; neither she nor the other girls knew how he'd take things. At times, he'd fly into a rage at the slightest provocation; at others, he'd talk gently and lucidly on any topic that caught his fancy. Just the other day, he'd stood in the garden for almost forty-five minutes expounding on the Latin names of the new plants and how best to tend to them.

"Oh, nothing, Doctor," Grace replied, wary. "I was just reading."

She moved, as if to step past him, but he shifted his weight and leaned in towards her.

"Well, I think we both know that isn't true," he said, dropping his voice as the distance between them shortened. "I assume you're looking this up because of Olivia's treatment. Something you overheard, perhaps? I see you seeing, Grace. You're a very observant girl."

There was no point trying to get out of the conversation; she knew that. So she decided instead to take advantage of his more talkative mood.

"What are the side-effects of the treatment?" she asked – sounding bold, but feeling anything but.

"Side effects! Yes, very good!" The doctor was suddenly, unexpectedly enthusiastic – pacing back and forth in front of Grace, his hands clasped behind his back and his head in the air, looking every bit like a lecturer delivering a talk to a group of students. "In the short term – drowsiness, headaches, nausea, confusion, aching muscles, loss of appetite." He continuing rattling off his list, then launched into the longer-term effects: "...difficulty concentrating, loss of creativity and energy, apathy, loss of emotional responses...though of course not *all* patients suffer these symptoms. Some people," he added with a flourish, "have no side effects at all."

"Didn't Belle die from a seizure?" Grace said. "What if Olivia dies while you're treating her?"

"That's very unlikely. But Grace, we must weigh up the good and the bad.

Olivia has what you might think of as... competing voices in her head. And I'm sure you've noticed the scarring on her arms? Some of these voices she hears tell her to hurt herself. It is my job to try to help her – and since I believe I *can* help her, don't you think I *should*?"

"Well, yes, of course. But how do you know any of this will work?"

Dr Baker sighed. "Those of us who want to make a difference in this world must be prepared to take risks, Grace. We must be willing to push the boundaries in order to advance."

"At what cost, though?"

"At any cost. There is no cost too great, where progress is at stake."

"**L**ook, I'll get it – you don't have to keep calling here. In fact, I'd like you to *stop* calling here." Father Jameson sounded stressed.

By the study door, Grace paused, the priest's afternoon tea still in her hand – not wanting to interrupt his phone call, and wanting moreover to hear what else he had to say.

"I don't appreciate your tone," he continued. "I know what I owe you, and I have some business in place to pay you back...Yes... yes, of course. What about instalments? I should have other... business reaching fruition in the next week or two. Yes? Alright. Very well. Until then."

He slammed down the receiver, and the force of the gesture startled her, causing the little silver tray she was holding – complete with the priest's cup of tea and cream slice – to sway and rattle.

"Who's out there? Is that you, Baker? Get in here, we need to talk numbers."

"Oh, no Father, it's me, Grace. I'm just bringing your afternoon tea. I'm sorry to interrupt." Grace stepped into the room, but was careful not to stray too far from the doorway.

The priest stared at her for a moment. "Grace." His voice mellowed. "Come in, dear, and put the tray down."

She walked across to the large oak desk and placed down the tray on top of it, gently. She should leave, she thought; the atmosphere was awkward, and would only become more so if she remained where she was. But then Father Jameson spoke again.

"I'm not sure what you heard there, my child," he said, "but it's nothing to worry about. And indeed, nothing to repeat to others."

"Of course," she told him, hurriedly – her desire to leave increasing with every second that passed. "I didn't really hear anything anyway, Father. I hope all is well."

"Yes, thank you, Grace. You may go."

She wanted to tell Ellen what she'd heard, was desperate to. But she had to wait. They had reading time all afternoon, but Sister Angela would be present throughout, and it wouldn't be sensible, Grace knew, to share any of what she'd learned in the nun's presence. Then they'd prepare dinner before sitting down to eat, and after *that,* clean up. Only when they'd readied themselves for bed, and Grace was alone with Ellen in the front upstairs bedroom, would any meaningful conversation be possible.

"Today was so strange," she began, when finally they *were* alone together. "This afternoon I heard Father Jameson having this... bizarre conversation on the telephone. It sounded like someone was asking for money from him. He told me not to mention it to anyone."

"Really?" Ellen was sitting cross-legged on her bed, directly across from Grace. "Maybe the rumours are true."

"Which ones?" Grace shifted her own body until her posture mirrored Ellen's.

"You know. Where he got himself into trouble with gambling debts. Apparently he owed some men money – some dubious men – so he took the money for the church roof, but then he lost all that, too. I guess he was trying to pay them off, but ended up with nothing."

"Do you think he and Dr Baker are involved in something illegal?" Grace bit her lip. "I wonder how they met, how Baker came to be here."

Ellen shook her head. "I never really believed the gambling stuff. He's a man of God, isn't he?"

"Well, at the moment he just sounds like a man with his back against a wall, and you know what *they're* capable of."

Ellen looked concerned. "What?"

"Anything, that's what. They're capable of anything."

CHAPTER 13

2018

"I think she's lovely, that Susan, I really do, but come on – it's a lot." Jessica was brushing her teeth, her hip resting on the edge of the sink. She looked in the mirror and back at Nicole, standing directly behind her. "Maybe it's an attention thing? We're new here, and I'm busy with work, so she's reeled you in with these...ghost stories." Jessica spat out her toothpaste and ran the back of her hand over her mouth.

"I'm not saying I believe all of it one hundred percent," said Nicole. "But I think *she* does. What I mean is, I think she's genuine in what she's saying."

Jessica turned around. "I'm not sure that makes it any better. Not if our options are either that she's lying for attention, or she believes in ghosts and is – for want of a more PC term – batshit crazy."

Nicole raised an eyebrow. "Yeah, I guess that's pretty much it. But either way, she's a nice woman. You don't have to talk to her if she bothers you, but I like her."

"Fine." Jessica smiled, and planted a minty kiss on her wife's lips. "Keep your weird friend. But right now – come to bed with me?"

Nicole woke up and stretched, her hand pressed against Jessica's sleeping body. She scooched over in the bed and put her arms around her, snuggling into Jess's back; placed a hand on Jess's stomach.

It was wet.

She withdrew it immediately, as quickly as if she'd been burned, and stared down at her fingers. The flimsy curtains allowed enough light into the room for her to discern the shape and colour of the objects in her field of vision: the illumination a mix of natural and artificial, the moon and the streetlight working together to keep the dark at bay. And in that light, she saw it: blood, *fresh* blood, an inky crimson dripping from her palm, already tacky in the crease between her index finger and thumb

"Jess! Jess wake up, wake up!"

She was shouting, but didn't care; didn't care about much of anything in that moment, except that her wife was bleeding. Bleeding and unconscious.

The body beside drew itself up to a seated position, its back still turned. When it moved, the motion was awkward, disjointed – a mannequin brought to life by a novice puppeteer. Slowly, *unnaturally* slowly, the head began to turn – farther around than the confines of any normal human ought to have allowed.

It wasn't Jess. It was – just as it had been, that night in the bathroom – someone else entirely.

The girl on the bed had long blond hair – but it was dark in places, and matted. With blood? Her eyelids were closed, as if she were asleep.

Her movements still jerky, still awkwardly stiff, she rose from the bed and faced Nicole. She didn't open her eyes – but still, Nicole felt, she was staring at her, through her. Slowly, the girl raised her hands to the side of her face and began scratching at something there, on the skin or under it.

Nicole couldn't look away; was horribly transfixed by what she was seeing, fear and revulsion churning in her gut as the girl pulled – *tugged* – at a piece of thread that hung from her cheek with the tips of fingers that seemed to have rotted half away. The girl struggled to keep hold of the thread – and, frustrated, began instead to claw at her eyes, picking at them frantically.

After a moment, the thread fell away, and she stopped, lowering her hands to her side, and giving Nicole a glimpse of her face.

Nicole screamed, or thought she did.

The girl's eyes were gone; had been ripped from their sockets, leaving nothing but pulpy red voids in the empty cavities of the sockets. And the thread, bloody now, and loose, but still partially attached to the skin they'd been holding closed.

Her eyes had been sewn shut.

Someone had sewn *them shut.*

There was blood on the front of her nightdress; the same dark, fresh blood Nicole could see now on her own hand. In the girl's hand, something glinted. A knife? A piece of glass?

No, Nicole saw; it was a teaspoon. The girl was holding a little teaspoon in her hand.

"My name is Belle," she said. "And this is my room, but I'm not allowed to sleep."

"Where's Jessica?" Nicole asked her – shaky, but audible. "My wife – where's my wife? What have you done with her?"

"She's in the other room." Belle said.

"Nicole? Who are you talking to?"

Jessica was standing, suddenly, at the bedroom door.

"Jess – oh my God, are you okay?" Relief poured from Nicole at the sight of her, but it was short lived; the pounding of her own heart reminding her they were both still in danger. She turned her attention back to the girl by the bed, and answered her wife's question as calmly as she was able. "I'm talking to Belle. Susan told us about Belle, remember?"

Jessica came fully into the room and positioned herself beside Nicole, silently taking her hand. There was a smell of talcum powder in the air again, Nicole noticed; choking, suffocating. Then it was gone.

"Why are you here, Belle?" Nicole asked, squeezing Jess's hand.

"You have to help them," Belle said. "They're downstairs, and you have to get them out."

"Who? Who's downstairs?" A wave of nausea rippled through Nicole's stomach. The air was clouded again, as if filled with smoke – then cleared, as quickly as it had come

Belle was gone.

And then it was only Nicole and Jessica again: the two of them alone together in the night.

Susan was standing by the sink, pouring more hot water onto a bed of teabags – their second pot of the morning.

After Belle had delivered her cryptic message, Nicole had run downstairs and searched every room in the house, looking for *them* – whoever *they* might be. She'd found no one. Eventually she'd given up the search: sat on the bottom step of the stairs and held her head in her hands for a moment, then taken out her phone and texted Susan. It was the middle of the night, so she hadn't expected a response. But against all odds, her phone had pinged a moment later.

I'm on my way over, Susan had said. *Put the kettle on.*

And, true to her word, she'd been at the front door a few moments later – still wearing pyjamas, a long brown coat thrown over them.

"Are you alright, dear?" she'd asked. "You said you'd met Belle – was it bad?"

"Well, it wasn't great." Nicole closed the door behind Susan and gestured her through to the kitchen. "Come through and have a cup of tea."

Now, deep into their second pot, Nicole had calmed slightly.

"It was horrifying, to be honest. I know you mentioned her, but I wasn't prepared for... that."

"It's the eyes," Susan said, knowingly.

"It's the *lack* of eyes, yes."

Susan hesitated. "And where was Jessica during all this?"

"Well, right now she's back in the bed – but she was out of the room when it happened, and Belle was lying on her side of the bed."

"Out of the room? Like in the bathroom?"

Nicole thought for a second. "Yeah, I guess so. I didn't ask her."

"So, she saw Belle? Because you said she didn't see Olivia, before."

"Yeah, she saw Belle. Do you think she's becoming more susceptible to the ghosts now?"

Susan nodded. "It would seem so, wouldn't it? You said her father died recently?"

"Yes, a few months back. She wasn't in a great way when it happened, but she's been doing better."

"Has she?" Susan didn't sound convinced. "Well that's good. It can't have been easy for her...or you."

"Well, yeah – I guess it was hard for us both. But mainly I just had to be there for Jess, you know? That was my job, to look after her, keep her safe."

"Right." Susan sat down at the table and busied herself freshening their cups with more steaming tea. "I never met my parents," she said, out of the blue.

Nicole had her cup almost to her mouth, but set it down again at this. "Oh, I'm so sorry – that must have been difficult."

"It was and it wasn't, I suppose. It's difficult to miss what you've never had. I mean I had parents, but they weren't my birth parents." Susan sounded wistful; lost in memory, her fingers fiddling with her necklace as she spoke. "Family is a funny thing, isn't it? It doesn't matter what we're given, we end up creating our own anyway."

"I guess that's true. Friends, partners, all of it. You were adopted, then?"

"Yes, straight from birth. 1955. My birth mother was young, single, and it was...frowned upon, back then. More than frowned upon, really; young women were sent away from their families, packed off to nunneries and homes for unwed mothers. Hard to believe now." Susan looked up at Nicole and smiled, faintly. "Anyway, Ireland's come a long way since."

Nicole wasn't sure what to say, so said nothing, and an easy silence descended on the table.

"This belonged to my mother," Susan said looking down at the chain she was toying with – holding it out from her chest for Nicole to see. "My adoptive mother, Annie... she gave it to me when I turned sixteen."

Nicole leaned in to look more closely at the pendant. It looked like a marble cross, she thought – but the shape was unusual. Crooked, somehow. "It's beautiful," she said.

"It's a St Brigid's cross," Susan told her. "Made from silver and Connemara marble. There's a crack running through it, always has been, but it's never broken, not in all these years. Just a little fracture," she said, running her finger over the damaged marble, "but sure, we all have those. Have you been out to Connemara yourself?"

"Jessica brought me out there once. It's beautiful – so wild and untamed."

"It's exactly that, untamed. Anyway. Annie said she got it from a nun, the cross – when I was young. Said it was from my birth mother. A gift, I assume. Something to remember her by, maybe."

"Did you ever try to find her?" Nicole didn't want to pry but was curious, nonetheless.

"No. I don't even know her name. Records weren't kept well back then, and what little were kept have been destroyed over the years, misplaced or washed out and faded in damp cabinets."

"I'm sorry, Susan."

"I've got this, though." She fingered the cross. "And I think about her sometimes – the life she might've led after she gave me up. I hope she was happy. I hope she lived wild and untamed herself."

"I'm sure she did." Nicole placed a hand over Susan's and squeezed, gently. "I'm sure she did just that."

CHAPTER 14
1955

O livia's behaviour was getting more erratic by the day, and the other girls were increasingly uneasy in her presence. Sometimes it was small things, things easy enough to ignore: mumbling to herself, or staring blankly into space. At other times, though, she was more violent – hitting herself, or throwing dinner plates at the walls.

"I thought the therapy was supposed to *help* her, not make her worse," Ruth whispered to Grace one morning, as they stood preparing eggs for breakfast in the kitchen.

"I'm telling you, he's guessing," Grace said. "Baker – he's just trying things out. Why else would he be practising here? And *he's* changed, have you noticed that? He's... twitchy, and he's popping more pills himself than he's giving to Olivia and Sinead combined. He sounds like a money box, rattling when he walks."

"Oh, come on! You're exaggerating. Besides, he told me he had a headache when I saw him taking medicine the other day."

"Well, he must get a lot of headaches, then. And if he's this amazing doctor, why is he in a town in Ireland working at a home for unwed mothers? This isn't even a doctor's surgery. He's just... in a house. And you know what we all have in common? Our families turning their backs on us. There's no one to check up on us, Ruth, and I'm telling you now...something's not right."

"Okay. Fine. Say he isn't who he's meant to be – what are *we* supposed to do about it? We're powerless, here Grace. We can't just run off."

"Why not?" Grace asked.

"Come on." Ruth ran a hand over her swollen belly. "Where am I going to go? How would I survive? And anyway, what about Olivia and Sinead? You'd just leave them here, would you? You think we're in danger, but it's grand to just sacrifice them? Jesus. What's your plan, exactly? For you and Ellen to run off into the sunset together?" Ruth had abandoned the whispering now; her voice was close to a roar.

"Now hang on, Ruth, that's not what I was saying at all. I just think we nee—"

"What's going on in here? I could hear your racket from the sitting room," said Sister Angela from the doorway. "Do you think it's acceptable to be in here arguing with one another?"

"I'm sorry, Sister." Grace wanted to defuse the situation as quickly as possible; the last thing she *or* Ruth ought to be doing was drawing attention to themselves. "We weren't fighting, just...debating something. We're sorry for disrupting you."

"Debating something, were you? It would behoove you both to be getting the breakfast ready and keeping your opinions to yourself. And Ruth, you should know better."

"Yes, Sister Angela," Ruth said. "Sorry, Sister Angela."

Apparently mollified, the nun turned and hobbled out of the kitchen.

"Look, Ruth," Grace started, her voice dropping again. "I'm not saying we leave anyone behind. But we *do* need to do something, and soon."

"Fine," Ruth said. "But just promise me you won't do anything rash, alright? Don't go putting yourself or anyone else in danger."

"I won't," Grace said. "I promise."

The day proceeded just as any other. The girls cleaned up after breakfast, and went, as usual, to spend a few hours in the reading room. It was coming up on noon when Sister Angela returned – to announce the day as her last in the house, and that Sister Tabitha would be returning to her post the next day.

Grace was delighted, though took pains not to let her pleasure show, at least in the company of Sister Angela. She'd missed Sister Tabby; had missed the sense that somebody cared, for her and for the other girls at Montpellier Street.

"As it's my last day," Sister Angela continued, "I thought we could all go outside and do some gardening. Wouldn't that be nice?"

A few days beforehand, several large bags of soil and four tall wooden flower boxes – each one at least two feet high – had been delivered to the front of the house. Dr Baker, it seemed – in one of his more lucid moods, perhaps – had decided a spot of horticulture might be just what the girls needed to keep them calm.

They filed outside, Sister Angela rattling off a laundry-list of instructions which Grace suspected had come directly from Baker.

"Alright, girls," she told them. "There are bags of soil over there beside the wooden planters. In the paper bags, you'll find an assortment of seeds; now, *they* have little notes with them to describe their own particular flower, as well as instructions on how deep the seed should be set into the soil, so read them carefully. Dr Baker said you can move the planters anywhere you want in the garden – make each one your own little space. There are only four, mind, so two of you will have to share."

"Why are they being so nice to us?" Ellen asked Grace, under her breath.

"I don't know," Grace said, her scepticism rising, "but they never do anything *just* to be nice."

It was lovely to be outside, though. And while Sister Angela sat sunning herself in an old fold-out chair and intermittently leafing through the *Galway Guardian*, the girls began to garden: helping each other move the planters out onto the grass, so they could get started.

Grace placed her own planter right beside Ellen's.

Ellen looked up and smiled. "You're not putting that there, are you?" She nodded down at the planter.

"Why not? They said to put it wherever we wanted...and I want mine here."

"But it won't look right," Ellen said, suppressing a laugh.

"What does *right* look like?" Grace asked her.

"You know...like, what people expect from a garden."

Grace leaned into Ellen and whispered in her ear. "I don't care what people expect and I don't care if it doesn't look right." She leaned back. "Besides: you don't want my flowers planted beside yours for the rest of time?"

"The rest of time?" Ellen scoffed.

"Until we leave here, at any rate." Grace watched the smile fade away from Ellen's face, darkening her eyes – and hated herself, suddenly, for bringing about the change in Ellen's mood. "What did I say?" she added.

"When? When do you think we will leave here?"

Grace let out a small sigh. "When we turn eighteen, I guess. We'll be adults then, and can do what we please."

"What will we do, though? How will we do it?" Ellen sounded fraught – the worry Grace guessed she must have been pushing deeper and deeper down inside herself now bubbling uncontrollably to the surface.

"Whatever it is, we'll do it together." Grace took Ellen's hand, holding her gaze. "We'll get out of here, we'll see and do everything, and we'll do it all together, okay?"

Ellen gave Grace's hand a squeeze. "Okay."

The front door opened, and Father Jameson and Dr Baker descended the steps. Ellen dropped Grace's hand, quickly, and they busied themselves with their planters.

"Afternoon ladies, lovely day for it," Father Jameson said, with a nod of his nicotine-stained head.

The men climbed into the black Jaguar currently parked outside the house – pristine and shone to a high polish, as always – and reversed out of the drive, starting off towards town.

This is it, Grace told herself. *This is the time to go into the house and see what you can find.*

She turned around to look at Sister Angela, whose eyes were now closed. The nun's mouth hung slightly open, and she appeared to be snoring, very gently.

She's asleep.

Sinead, Grace saw, was actually planting her seeds – while Ruth was over with Olivia, helping her even out the soil and pick which seeds to plant.

Grace turned back to Ellen. "I'm going to nip inside," she said quietly. "See if I can find anything in Father Jameson's study."

"Oh, God – that doesn't sound safe, Grace." Ellen, who fell asleep most nights listening to Grace's theories on Father Jameson and Dr Baker and what the two of them might be up to in the house, couldn't hide her concern.

"It'll be fine," Grace said. "I'll be fast, and I'll be able to hear the car if they come back early. And if Sister Angela wakes up and asks where I am, you can just say I'm in the bathroom."

"I don't like this," Ellen told her, with a forlorn shake of her head. "At all. But I don't think that's going to matter much, is it? So just be careful, alright? Be careful, and be quick."

Up the steps Grace went: through the front door and right, into Father Jameson's study. Her first observation was that he could do with opening a window; a musty smell of body odour hung in the air, cut through with more than a hint of stale alcohol. The sun pierced the net curtains, but did little more than showcase the dust that spiralled in the spears of light Grace dispersed as she crossed the floor to the priest's large desk.

She lowered herself down onto the leather-bound chair behind it and pulled open the narrow desk drawer to her left. Inside were dozens of yellow slips of paper: betting slips.

So the rumours were true. He really was a gambler.

She closed the drawer and pulled open a larger one directly below it, which held nothing but paper folders. She pulled one out and set it on the desk. There were clippings inside, newspaper clippings: all from English Newspapers, and all from 1953.

The Chronicle – 29th of May, 1953
The discovery of Rapid Eye Movement (REM) sleep has been brought to light by researchers Alphonso Amaleto and Nathaniel Wrightman for the very first time. Research continues into our sleep cycles, and psychologists continue to debate the purpose of dreaming.

Why has he kept these? she wondered. *What has this got to do with anything?*

She read on, unable to stop – turning her attention to another of the clippings.

The study had been delayed, after one of the researchers, a Dr Charles Baker, had his licence to practice medicine revoked following accusations of unethical practice. No further details were available at the time of going to print.

Jesus.

Grace stood up, still holding the paper, and fanned out another dozen or so across the desk, each one telling a similar story.

He's not even a doctor anymore, she told herself. But why did Father Jameson have the clippings in his desk?

Insurance: it's an insurance policy. He doesn't trust Baker either.

She folded one of the clippings and put it carefully into her sock. She closed the folder and placed it back into the drawer; pushed it closed and got to her feet. She was walking towards the door when she saw the key: heavy and tarnished brass, hanging from the wall near the light switch. She took it down and held it in the palm of her hand, knowing immediately what it was for; that it would match only one door in the house. The door to the basement.

The keyhole there was much larger than those belonging to the other doors in Montpellier Street. Grace herself had stopped to look through it more than once – finding nothing but pitch black beyond.

She closed her hand around the key, feeling the weight of it in her sweating palm, and left the study, turning right down the hall. Just before the kitchen, she stopped – directly in front of the basement door.

It's now or never, isn't it?

She slid the key into the lock and turned her wrist. The door creaked open, revealing a small alcove just deep enough to hold a mop, a bucket and a bottle of Jeyes Fluid, and beside it a short, narrow staircase leading down into darkness. She hesitated, but only for a moment – then, pushing away her fear, began her descent.

She fumbled along the wall for the light switch and flicked it on. The door closed behind her as the bare bulb above her head sprung to life, throwing harsh, flickering strobe light over the stairs, the bare brick walls... and the basement below.

There was a metal table down there, she saw, in the very centre of the room – furnished with leather restraints to tie down anyone unlucky enough to be secured there at the wrists and ankles. She couldn't make out much else, from the top of the stairs – but knew immediately that going down them any further would be a horrible mistake. Despite how'd she'd felt earlier, she didn't want to be there *now*.

She turned back to the door and twisted the handle, but it didn't open, not an inch. Her fingers scrambled for the key in her cardigan pocket – but when she looked up at the place where the keyhole should have been, saw nothing there. Dread built low in her stomach, acid rising up her throat; she ran a hand over the door, but felt only smooth, unbroken wood under her palm.

She glanced upwards, her eyes searching for something, anything, that might give her some clue about what was happening – some sense of how a lock that had been there on one side of the door could possibly be absent on the other.

And there—near the very top of the door, only inches from the head — was the keyhole. *A* keyhole, at least. One an altogether different shape to the key in her hand, requiring an entirely different key.

CHAPTER 15

2018

From the top step of the house, looking out onto the front garden, Nicole could not only see but *feel* the weeping willow tree looming over her – and couldn't help but recall the story of the priest who, as Susan told it, had committed suicide there. She felt less strongly about it than she suspected she ought to – which made her feel odd, though she also suspected *odd* was starting to lose all meaning to her, of late. It had been two days since Belle had made an appearance, and Nicole had expected to find herself on edge – or, perhaps, making plans to move out of the house altogether. Instead, she felt strangely at home; strangely settled on Montpellier Street. Susan called round every day, full of baked goods and gossip; Jessica was working on her website, trying to win new clients; and between them, they were sorting the house, slowly but surely.

She stepped back inside, into the kitchen.

"Today," she announced, "I am tackling that garden."

"Yeah?" Jessica turned around from the sink, a sceptical grin plastered across her face.

"Yes. I'm serious this time. I have a plan; I'm going to finish off weeding those randomly placed raised beds, then I'm going to cut the lawn and at some point—though, okay, maybe not today—I'll trim the hedges along the side."

"Well, you sound like a woman on a mission, I'll give you that. One problem, though—we don't have a lawn mower yet."

Nicole walked over to the kettle and flicked it on. "True. But we have a Susan. She must have one, or her son Michael will. I'll pop 'round to her after I do the beds."

Jessica laughed. "As if you'll get the chance to go round. She'll be outside and over to chat to you the second that front door closes. If she wasn't in her sixties, I'd be keeping my eye on you two."

"Stop! She's just lonely, and it's not like she has much else to do. Besides, I enjoy her."

The kettle boiled, steam billowing from the spout. Nicole filled her cup, added a teabag and lost herself momentarily in the swirl of the water as it infused.

"Fine," Jessica said. "But speaking of not having much to do – have you thought about going back to work?"

Nicole hesitated. "Not yet. Another couple of weeks, maybe; I'm enjoying my extended leave. Besides, baby, it's accounting. No one's in a rush to go back to that."

Sipping her tea, she leaned back against the counter – and felt the left pocket of her jeans vibrate. Just before the ringtone could kick in, she took out her phone, silenced it and returned it to the pocket, then took another gulp of tea before setting down the cup.

"Was that your sister?" Jessica asked, accusatory.

Nicole nodded.

"You need to call her. Seriously, it's getting weird, you're avoiding her."

"I will! I'll call her. It's not a big deal; she just always seems to get me at a bad time. If I call her back now, we'll be on for an hour and I won't get the garden done. I love her, I do, but she'll just be complaining about not getting enough rest because Ronan isn't in his sleep routine yet, or something." She stepped closer to Jessica and nuzzled at her neck. "Please don't make me. I want to go outside and play."

"Fine – go and play, you big baby." Jessica pushed her away – but gently. "You'll have to speak to her soon, though. I'll make sure of it, if it's the last thing I do."

Outside, the weather was overcast: the clouds above moving like wax in a lava lamp, slowly churning. Nicole got stuck into the flowerbeds immediately.

She'd call over to Susan about the lawn mower, she decided, when she'd finished. But she'd got barely halfway through the weeding when Susan's head appeared over the wall.

"Morning love, grand day for it. How's the inside getting on? Still much to do?"

Susan rounded her little white wall and made her way into Nicole's front garden, pulling on a pair of gardening gloves as she walked.

"It's slow going inside," Nicole shouted back at her. "I think I prefer being outdoors."

"You're the same as myself, so. I do like being out in the garden. What's the plan for today, then?"

Before Nicole had time to reply, Susan was standing right there next to her, examining the planters.

Nicole gestured back with her hands. "Well, I've almost finished these flower boxes, but, actually, I was going to ask you a favour."

"Anything, love. How can I help?"

"Would you have a lawn mower, by any chance?"

"Well, ours packed in there a week or so back, but Michael has one, I believe. I'll have him call round to do the grass for you – save you the bother, when you've the whole house to be sorting. Besides, weren't you to get him to look at that wiring? Have you smelled any more burning since?"

"I still get it occasionally," Nicole admitted. "Mainly at night. But with all the goings-on... it's taken a bit of a back seat, you know?"

"Understandable. And how are the ghosts? Any more sign of them?"

"No, actually – things have been quiet the last day or two. Which *sounds* good, but makes me worry we might be due another visitor sooner rather than later."

"Oh, don't think like that, love. Sure, they'll come and go as they please. And they haven't done you any harm, have they? Now tell me: how's Jessica this weather? Has she got that web thing going yet?"

Nicole was faintly appalled.

"They might not have done us any harm," she said, "but they've scared the shit out of us." Nicole caught Susan's disapproval at the curse. "Sorry, Susan. But anyway, yes – Jess is all good, working away. She's busy all day, though, so that hasn't helped with getting the place in order."

"Oh, I should come over tomorrow and get stuck in with you. That would be perfect. Jessica can work away upstairs—we won't bother her—and you and I can get the place spick and span."

Susan was brimming with enthusiasm; it was hard for Nicole not to be swept up in it.

"Okay, okay, yeah. If you're sure, let's do it."

Susan had a hint of The Borg about her, she thought; resistance was indeed futile.

"Sure I'm sure," Susan told her. "Oh, I can bring my new kitchen spray; it's a wonder, so it is. I'll give our Michael a ring later and tell him to bring the lawnmower 'round. But it'll probably be tomorrow, too – is that okay for you, love?" She didn't wait for Nicole to respond before continuing. "Grand. That's that sorted, so." She clapped her hands together. "Right then – where are we? Will I start this one over here?"

She wandered across to the nearest of the raised beds and began to rip away at the weeds.

"You don't have to help," Nicole said – aware even as she spoke that her protest would do nothing to stop Susan in her tracks. "You've been so good already."

"Nonsense, love. Besides, I like to be out in the air. I go a bit mad if I stay in the house all day."

Susan couldn't afford to get much madder, Nicole thought. So perhaps it was best just to let her help out.

"Do you want to try and move these, so the four are spaced out equally?" Susan was eyeing up the raised flowerbeds. "They could do with a lick of paint too, if you don't mind me saying. I've some white in the shed, would that suit you?"

"I think I'll leave them where they are," Nicole said. "I assume they're like that for a reason. No point in moving them apart now if we don't have to. And I think I like that they're...off. White might be nice, though."

Susan smiled. "Alright, then. I'll nip home when we've done these and get the paint. We can sort them after lunch."

"Perfect." Nicole threw more weeds onto the little pile.

"Oh, I meant to say to you." Susan sounded excited, suddenly. "I dug out some of that research I mentioned, from when I was looking into this house."

Nicole's eyes widened. "And what did you find out? Full disclosure: I've done zero research. I was going to go down to the library and see what I could find out, but..."

"Well, you can still do that, of course. But what I have might be even more useful."

"Which is?"

"A name." Susan said. "And a rumour. Or more like... half a rumour, I suppose you'd say."

"Whose name?" Nicole leaned back against the flower planter, her arms folded.

"So, we knew…" The older woman halted, mid-sentence. "You know," she said, "we should really be having tea for talk like this."

"Susan!"

"Alright, love – alright. So, we knew there was the priest here, didn't we? Father Jameson. But we can't get much info on him, because…well…" Susan glanced meaningfully up at the weeping willow.

Nicole followed the trajectory of the look, trying not to dwell too long on the priest who'd once been hanging there. "Right."

"But now we have another name – Sister Tabitha Ryan. She only lived in this house briefly, but when she left, she left the vocation altogether. Just… chucked it in, the being a nun. So, *I* think she might know something." Susan's smile widened; she was practically beaming with pride.

"But where *is* she?" Nicole said. "Who gave you her name? And what is it you think she knows? Wait – is she even alive now?"

Susan's smile faded. "Well… it was the postman who told me about her, because he knows the whole country and I was asking him about the house. It was a big scandal in the area, apparently, when our Sister Ryan left the nuns. 1955 it was, he said, and she was only a young one, twenty or twenty-one, so she'd be about…eighty-four-ish now, I suppose. Where she is, exactly… I'm not sure. She was from around here originally, but it seems she headed away to England after… whatever it was that happened. She did come back at some point, though, so the postman said."

"I guess it's a start. I could look her up and see what I find out."

Susan smiled. "That's more like it! Now we have a lead."

Nicole laughed. "We *might* have a lead. And we *might* have a dead ex-nun somewhere. We'll see."

They returned to weeding out the planters. It was nice to be out in the air, getting her hands dirty, Nicole thought; unexpectedly relaxing. When the flowerbed was free of weeds, she began to till the soil with the hand trowel – digging in and out of the earth, hypnotised by the motion of her own body, her own arm.

Which, she realised with a start, looked suddenly, horribly different than it should: the flesh there twisted and gnarled. An angry red scar bubbled and fizzed up under the skin of her left forearm, rippling, becoming a raised length of fibrous tissue seven inches long.

She screamed; clawed at herself, at the limb she no longer recognised as her own.

Somewhere nearby, Susan was calling for her; shouting. But the words were unintelligible, drowned out by the deafening tsunami of her panic.

Nicole stumbled backwards, falling flat onto her back. She found herself staring up at the weeping willow's canopy – and within it the swaying body of the priest, staring back at her with bulging eyes and a blue tongue protruding, flaccid, from his mouth,. Thick, knotted rope dug into his purple neck, his face red and strained with what must have been the effort he'd made at breathing.

She choked on her breath at the sight of him; jumped back to her feet, and looked instinctively down at her arm.

The scar had vanished: her arm was her own again, only a freckle or two marking the skin. She ran her other hand up and down it the forearm, squeezing her eyes open and closed, daring herself to look back up at the tree. When eventually she *did* look, she saw it was empty: there was no priest there, no rope. Just snippets of rolling clouds framed by the willow's branches – moving faster now, threatening a change of weather.

What the fuck?

"Nicole?" Susan said, the words clearer this time.

Nicole knew, right then, she wouldn't tell her what she'd seen: the hanging man, the disappearing scar. *Couldn't* tell her. The last thing she needed was Susan thinking she'd lost her mind.

"I'm sorry," she answered, as slow and calm as she could manage. "It was a...a spider, I think. On my wrist. Gave me a fright."

Susan had one hand on her heart; the other propping her up against the flower box. "Jesus Christ, love, you gave me an awful fright. I thought you'd seen the Banshee or something."

"Language, Susan," Nicole told her, automatically – trying, for the second or third or twentieth time in as many days to tamp down her shock, the growing fear in her belly. Her heart betrayed her though, pounding a hammer in her chest.

How far exactly, she wondered, were the ghosts of Montpellier Street prepared to go, to get her attention?

CHAPTER 16

1955

There was no way out, Grace thought. She was trapped down there, in the basement.

Panic washed over her at the prospect. Dr Baker and Father Jameson would be back soon, she knew. And what would they do to her, if they found her? The Doctor's mood swings were unpredictable, frightening, and the priest... well, he had his own concerns, didn't he?

She scanned the door again, searching in vain for a keyhole. Eventually, defeated, she turned and faced the stairs.

I guess the only way out is down.

She stepped down, down, down the steps, her eyes fixed on the metallic table ahead of her. When she reached the bottom step, the room seemed to open up, grow wider – revealing, to her dismay, no other possible escape route. There *was* natural light, though; that was coming in from somewhere, surely?

To the right she saw a small rectangular window, level with the ground outside. She walked across to it, examined it, but could see right away there was no way to open it; it was nothing more than a pane of glass set into the wood. There were no other windows in sight, no hidden doors or secret hatches.

Damn it.

The only way in or out of the room, it seemed, was via the door at the top of the stairs. She'd need to stay calm, then; need to think of a story to tell the men, a reason for her to be down there. Something plausible, believable.

She took a moment to properly consider the room; after all, she reasoned, she'd gone down there in the first place to investigate it, to see what it contained.

Silently, she catalogued its layout, its contents.

In the corner of the basement was a filing cabinet with six tall, metallic drawers. The walls around the door and stairway were bare brick – down in the main part of the basement, though, they were tiled white. Both the tiles and the room itself were neat and clean; everything looked spotless, nothing out of place. All the benches were made of a metal she couldn't readily identify – aluminium, perhaps. There were little white cabinets fixed to the walls, some with transparent glass doors; through them, she could make out pill bottles, a whole shelf of them, though recognised none of the names on the labels. Beside the ominous table was a squat silver trolley on casters, containing four trays of what appeared to be surgical instruments and syringes. Over to her right, she saw a small grate set into the floor— a drain.

So the whole room can be hosed down.

Something in the grate caught her eye: a stain, perhaps, conspicuous against the immaculate white of the tiles. She bent to get a better look; saw it *was* a stain, speckled reddish-brown, like rust.

She squinted, looking closer. There was something else there too, caught up in the stain. It looked like... hair, human hair; not from any one person, but in several different colours, a half-dozen shades of blonde and brown and auburn. With the long key she was holding, she prodded it; pulled a clump of the hair from the grate.

The smell of it. Mother of God, the smell of it...

She staggered backwards, dropping the key to the ground. Put a hand over her mouth and gagged, trying to breathe, to stop herself from throwing up. The smell rising up from the drain was rancid, utterly rancid. Clearly, she'd disturbed the stagnant waters there: she could almost taste the sulphuric rot of it, as if she were breathing in an open sewer. There was hair, still, wrapped around the key – but what she pulled up from the grate wasn't rust but blood. And lying in the middle of the matted, bloody hair itself was a fingernail: ripped and ragged, a portion of the nail-bed still attached; the tangled mass of hair a fishing net that had somehow dredged not buried treasure but a sunken abomination from the depths.

From somewhere outside came a crackling sound: the crunch of gravel under a wheel. The room darkened, and her eyes darted to the little rectangular window above her. She took another breath and held it; watched as the white-rimmed wheels of the black Jaguar rolled past the window and drew to a stop.

She got up off the ground and grabbed for the key. With it, she poked the clump of bloody hair and its stomach-churning catch back down into the darkness of the drain – one hand over her mouth as the mass slipped away, its horrors with it. She thought she heard the car's doors shut – then, a moment later, voices echoing through the entrance hall.

Think, she told herself. *You have to think, if you want to get out of here.*

In the dim light of the overhead bulb, she rushed towards the stairs, slowing her ascent as she felt the floorboards creak under her feet. The voices were getting louder now; Dr Baker and Sister Angela might have been directly outside the basement door.

Grace edged closer to the top of the stairs and clicked off the light switch – carefully, so carefully. The stairs and the basement were plunged again into darkness.

"Bring Olivia in from the garden," she heard the Doctor say. "We must begin today's treatment. I'll prep the room – just knock on the door when she's ready to come down."

Grace felt beads of cold sweat break the skin on the back of her neck. Any second, the locked door would open, leaving her with no option but to explain herself to a man she now believed – for what other conclusion could she draw, from the hair and blood and fingernails in the drain? – to be not only utterly deranged, but dangerous.

Out of the corner of her eye she spied the mop bucket, its upturned mop resting against the wall, and an idea struck her. She shimmied past it and pressed her back up against the wall, making herself as flat as possible and hiding her face behind the mop. She felt like her heart might beat out of her chest: the Doctor would be walking right past her at any moment, just inches away.

She closed her eyes – then opened them again at the sound of his key in the lock and the slight gust of air that followed as he yanked the door open. His hand reached towards her face, as if about to grab her; she could feel it, smell the rubbing alcohol on his fingers. But then, at the last minute, it changed course, and he flicked on the light. He was holding a letter, she saw, and appeared engrossed in it – walking right past her and down the stairs, seemingly oblivious to her presence. Only when she heard him begin to move the surgical table at the bottom of the stairs was she able to breathe again.

Yet, relieved though she was that she hadn't been discovered, she was, she realised, in much the same position as she'd been: trapped. She knew Olivia was on her way down, and that the door would open again; she just needed to be ready to run when it did. It would be her only chance of getting away, her only opportunity to escape.

She looked around at her feet, trying to find something – anything – she could use to jam the door open. It would need to be thin; thin enough that the door wouldn't look obviously ajar.

She could hear more footsteps in the hall; the doctor readying the room below. She'd have to act fast. In the deepest recesses of the alcove, she saw a cardboard box, containing what looked like four bottles of bleach. Pushing away thoughts of why there might be bleach there, and what it might have washed away, she bent down and gently tore one of the smaller side flaps from the box – then drew herself up to her full height again and waited for the basement door to open, the sliver of card shaking in her hand. She'd only have the briefest window to slip the piece of cardboard between the door and frame to stop it from closing.

Finally, the door opened and Olivia, unaccompanied, passed through it, pausing at the top of the stairs. The door began to close but Olivia seemed reluctant to move, to descend the stairs.

Please, Grace willed her, *just go.*

The door was still closing as Olivia at last took her first step down to the basement. With barely a second to go, Grace leaned forward and placed the card between the bolt and its strike plate in the wooden frame. Relief flooded her when it stuck; when the door stayed open. But the joy was short-lived.

There were other voices in the hall, other people out there. She couldn't leave, not yet – would have to bide her time before she could slip outside and make her excuses to Sister Angela, before she could confect some story or other about where she'd been. And what would happen to Olivia in that basement, once she left? What was happening to her now?

Grace had to know.

She hunkered down low and crept out to the top of the stairs; looked down, then immediately wished she hadn't.

Olivia was on the table. Grace could see only the upper half of her body, but it was clear Olivia's wrists were strapped, secured to the metal. There was something in her mouth, too: something black, plastic or rubber. She was... biting down on it, clamping it between her teeth.

Grace shifted position in hope of a better view – but in doing so, caught Olivia's attention. The girl looked right at her, her eyes widening in shock, and then turning to plead with her. The girls stared at one another for a moment, both of them trapped. The sense of connection was shattered, though, when

Olivia's eyes snapped closed and her body jerked abruptly, her shoulders rising from the table. She went rigid; seemed to hover briefly in the air before the full weight of her slapped back down onto the table. Her eyes flew open and fixed again on Grace – but were filled this time with frightened tears. She bit down on the black mouthpiece, white foam exuding from her mouth. Her body jerked a second time, and it was then Grace realised what she was seeing: an electric current, passing through Olivia's fragile body. She gasped; stifled the reaction with her hand.

She couldn't help. Couldn't speak out.

There was nothing to do but make her escape.

"What do you think happened down there?" Ellen asked.

They were in their bedroom, Ellen on her bed with her back against the wall and Grace beside her.

"I don't know," Grace said. "But there were different hair colours, a lot of them – which means more than one person. Who even knows how many girls have come through this house before we got here? They were renovating before I came, but we don't know how long the church owned this place before that. All we *do* know is that someone had their fingernail ripped out and it wasn't any of us." She let out a long, slow breath.

Ellen reached out a hand and placed it on Grace's. "It's okay. You're safe now."

"*For* now, you mean." Grace stood up and began to pace the floor. "You didn't see her face, El— her eyes, the pain."

Ellen untangled herself from the bed and pulled Grace close.

"It'll be alright. We'll get to the bottom of this. And when we do, we'll expose Baker for the fraud he is. I promise"

A loud crashing sound from somewhere outside interrupted their embrace. They pulled apart, holding each other at arm's length; listening for a follow-up noise that might explain the first. A soft thud came, and then... nothing.

Grace opened the door and stepped out into the hallway, Ellen following after her. Grace looked left, towards the bathroom: saw both light and steam escaping from under the door. The vapour rose, invading the landing like fog seeping over hills on a misty morning. She tiptoed towards the bathroom; the other bedroom door was slightly open, she noticed. She turned the handle of the bathroom door, afraid of what she'd find inside; paused, then pushed open the door, ever so slightly.

"Hello? Is everything okay in there?"

There was no response, though she hadn't expect there would be. She opened the door a little more, and was greeted on the other side by the sight of a broken mirror, its splintered reflections paving the floor onto which it had crashed. She stopped for a moment; studied a piece of the mirror, one that had landed in such a way as to cause it to stand upright, propped up against the wall – reflecting the inside of the bathroom.

She closed her eyes and steadied herself against the door.

Ellen, still behind her, was growing frustrated. "What? What is it? What can you see?"

"Go and get Dr Baker." Grace could hear it – the hopelessness in her own voice. The sad, sick knowledge that no amount of urgency would change what lay inside the room.

"No," Ellen said, standing firm. "I'm not going to that crazy man. What is it – what can you see? Show me." She nudged Grace aside, or tried to. But Grace wouldn't move. Didn't want her to see.

"Please," she told Ellen. "Just trust me – go and get the Doctor."

Ellen stopped pushing. "Okay," she conceded. "Okay. I'll get him." She spun around; headed back along the landing to wake Baker.

Grace couldn't bring herself to open the door any wider, much less to walk inside. She stared instead at the propped-up mirror, a portal to the horror within.

Olivia's eyes were reflected there, open wide but murky in death. Her neck had been slashed open; blood still seeped from the wound, beginning to congeal between the broken fragments of mirror on the floor. The shard she'd used to rip into her own flesh lay between her splayed fingers, sharp as a blade.

Two things stuck Grace, as she stared into Olivia's dead eyes.

The first was that Olivia would have watched herself die, would have seen it happen. She couldn't have planned it, of course; the position of the fallen mirror was random, a quirk of fate. But nevertheless, there it was – Olivia's blank stare trapped within its surface.

The second thing, Grace thought – flashing back to the basement, to Olivia strapped down on that table as her body convulsed—was that Olivia, too, had found a way to escape, in the end.

CHAPTER 17

2018

The bleat of the alarm brought Nicole, blinking and stirring, into the day. She reached out to her bedside locker and silenced it. She hadn't woken in the night, it seemed – which was in itself a bit of a novelty, of late.

She looked across the bed and saw Jess was still lying there: still fast asleep, her short dark hair sticking out at odd angles, her chest gently rising and falling. Nicole looked at her and smiled. She loved these quiet moment; moments of contentment, before the demands of the day encroached on their solitude. She could live in a world with Jess, and only Jess, and be completely happy; that was how she'd known she wanted to marry her, to spend the rest of her life with her.

She leaned over and kissed Jess's forehead – then, careful not to wake her, swung her legs out of the bed and rose, heading out onto the landing. She was halfway down the stairs, en route to a much-needed coffee, when she heard the doorbell ring.

Who the hell...? Susan; it has to be Susan.

She quickened her pace, making for the front door, and was confused upon opening it to be greeted with the sight of a stranger on her doorstep: a strapping, six-foot gentleman with a mop of red hair.

"Good morning," he told her, more cheerily than she might have expected. "You must be Nicole. I'm Michael, Susan's son, but you can call me Mick. Welcome to Montpellier Street."

He extended a shovel-like hand, and Nicole shook it, noting both the roughness of his skin and the gentleness of the handshake.

"Nice to meet you, Mick. You're up bright and early."

"Well, my mother said you needed your garden doing, and, sure, you know what she's like, all go, go, go. I hope I didn't wake you – I won't actually need to disturb you at all, it's a petrol mower." He gestured down to the lawnmower at the bottom of the steps. "I'll get going, so. And just to let you know, my mother will be 'round herself in half an hour. She was gathering cleaning supplies like a woman possessed, so consider yourself warned."

"Good to know. Thanks, Mick." She smiled at him, she hoped kindly. "Will you have a cup of coffee before you start?"

"I'm grand, thanks. I might pop up when I'm finished."

He turned and headed away from the house, down the steps, towards the garden and the lawnmower. He walked with a limp, she noticed; quite a pronounced one.

She closed the door and stepped back inside, her mind returning to coffee and toast. Less than 15 minutes later, Susan made her promised appearance.

"Good morning, good morning," she said, breezing into the kitchen with a black bag of cleaning products. "You're up, anyways – that's a start."

"You don't want a cuppa first?" Nicole was already reaching for the kettle.

"I had breakfast over at the house. Now up you get, love. We're squaring this house today, by hook or by crook."

When Nicole was suitably dressed for cleaning, the two of them started in the sitting room. There were boxes of books for Nicole to shelve; Susan, meanwhile, got to work dusting the surfaces.

"Any visitors in the night?" she asked.

"No, actually." Nicole picked up an illustrated hardback – one of Jess's

Discworld books. "It was a pretty restful night again. You think they got bored of us?"

Susan didn't laugh; didn't so much as crack a smile. "And Jess? Has she been okay, seen anything...unusual?"

"She's been fine. She was fast asleep when I was getting up. She works late a good bit – has clients in the States, so there's a time difference."

"Right."

"Actually, though, I was thinking about something last night. When Belle said *they need help* – what do you think she meant? And if she wanted something from me, why didn't she just ask me directly?"

Susan pondered this for a moment. "Well," she said, "they do say ghosts that died in a... let's call it a *traumatic* way might not be exactly capable of communicating in the way you and I understand it. More like they're... trapped in a loop. Reliving their trauma, over and over again."

"Jesus, that's grim."

"It's as if they're echoes, love. Reproductions of the souls of people who need to be released so they can rest."

"I thought you didn't believe in ghosts?"

Now Susan smiled. "Just because people don't believe in something, it doesn't mean that something doesn't exist."

"Profound," Nicole said, deadpan.

"You know," Susan replied, returning to her dusting, "if you cleaned as much as you talk, this place might be in better shape."

Nicole opted for a change of topic.

"Your son Michael," she said. "It's lovely of him to cut the lawn. I really appreciate how you're both helping me, helping us."

Susan softened. "Of course, love. It's what neighbours do. I hope you know that, that we're here for you. You're going through a difficult time – moving to a new house, and an unusual house at that. It's okay to...lean on people a bit."

It was surprising, Nicole thought: Susan's show of emotion, the dropping of her stoic guard. Though it didn't last long.

"Did you tell that son of mine to come in here and look at your wiring when he's finished with the lawn?" the older woman added.

"I did not."

"I'll remind him, then; we don't want this place going up in smoke, or ghosts will be the least of your problems."

"Did he hurt his leg?"

"What's that, love?"

"Michael. He was limping earlier – did he hurt his leg?'"

"You could say that." There was a long, considered pause – again, Nicole thought, quite unusual for Susan. "He was in a car accident, a few years ago now. Black ice, it was. The car skidded and lost control, rolled over a few times; he had to be cut out of it. Lucky to be alive, so he is."

"That's awful."

"He was in a bad way for a long time after. It wasn't just the rehabilitation – the nightmares were terrible, too."

"Poor guy." Nicole watched Michael through the window as he cut the lawn.

"He's doing well now, that's the main thing. It's strange, though – how the body breaks and heals, but the mind..."

"What do you mean?" Nicole asked, when it was clear Susan wouldn't be finishing the thought without some prompting.

"Well, with the mind... you never really know if it's mended. It's like a cut with a scab on it – the slightest pressure and the wound opens, then before you know it, it's bleeding again. Anyway, dear," she said – signalling, it seemed to Nicole, that no further meditations on the delicacy of the human psyche would be forthcoming, "these floors are a disgrace. Normally I'd offer to take my shoes off in a neighbour's house for fear of making them dirty, but with these I'd say it's the other way around."

"I have a mop out the back in the utility room," Nicole offered.

"Grand, so. Stay where you are, I'll get it. I think it's safe to say you don't know how it works."

Nicole went out front to chat to Michael and get some air, away from the smell of wood polish. He had finished with the lawn and taken it on himself to trim the hedges.

"Oh, hi." Seeing her, Michael put down the shears and wiped his forehead with the back of his hand. "You startled me there. How are things going inside?"

"Well, they're going. Your mother's certainly a force to be reckoned with."

"Don't I know it," he laughed. "She likes to stay busy." He shifted his weight from one side to the other, awkwardly.

Nicole nodded to Michael's leg. "Do you want to come in and sit down?"

"Oh, it's grand. I was in an accident a while back, that's all. It plays up now and then."

She couldn't have explained what, but something compelled her to ask Michael about his accident. "What was it?" she said. "What happened exactly?"

Susan passed through the kitchen on her way to the utility room, intent on unearthing a mop and bucket.

The smell hit her right away – so strong and so foul, there was nothing to do but cover her mouth and nose.

She pushed open the utility room door and peered in – her eyes widening in disbelief when she saw what Nicole had been keeping in there.

Things were bad, she realised. Worse even than she'd thought.

"It was a car accident," Michael said. "Single car collision, thankfully. Black ice on the road. I couldn't see it, obviously – and just like that, the car skidded off the road and just... rolled and rolled." He looked down at his injured leg, visibly shaken.

"God, I'm so sorry," said Nicole. "It must have been terrifying."

"Yeah, it was awful, but the worst thing was the shock, the confusion. It just happened so fast." He looked up at her; held her eye. "I know people always say that, but it's true – one minute you're driving along, and the next thing you know, you're hanging upside down from your seatbelt at the bottom of a ditch."

She sat back on one of the planters and sighed, scratching her arm. "I can only imagine. It must have been so scary, so disorienting."

"It really was. And then with the airbag and everything, I thought the car was on fire and I couldn't get out, couldn't see through the haze. I was full sure I was going to burn alive." He ran a hand over his face, as if checking the flesh there was still intact.

Nicole shook her head. "I'm so glad you're okay, that you got out. Did the car go up?"

"In flames? Oh no, there was no fire. It's a weird trick of the senses, you know? They put a little charge inside the airbag to make it go off on impact, create a sort of... mini explosion. But it smells like burning, and then there's all the powder in the air that looks like smoke... "

Nicole's brow furrowed. "The powder?"

"Yeah – when they pack the airbags, they cover them in talcum powder, get it right up in all the folds and grooves. It stops the bags from sticking to themselves when they release, so when they pop out— poof! Talcum powder everywhere." He readjusted his stance, redistributing his weight back to his other leg. "Since we're sharing war stories," he asked her, "mind if I asked what happened there?"

She followed his gaze down to her left forearm, the one she'd been scratching – to the long, half-healed scar that bisected the skin. The scar that had no right to be there.

She tensed; squeezed her eyes shut and willed it gone, just as she had that day in the garden. But when she opened them again, it was still there, as large and angry as it had been. A part of her; ineradicable.

H and still clasped across her nose and mouth, Susan entered the utility room and closed the kitchen door behind her – sealing herself inside with the source of the fetid smell.

It sat haphazardly along the countertop: minced meat, mound upon mound of it, some in plastic packaging and some in pink-stained paper butcher's bags, all of it rancid. The room itself buzzed with flies, the air around them heavy with animal decay.

The mince, she saw, seemed to be decomposing at different rates, like corpses on a body farm – some portions of it fresher and less rotten than the rest. Or perhaps it was simply that some of the bags were older; that the meat inside had been there longer. A few of the portions were bright red, bloody; others had been reduced to a yellowing slime, while others still had turned to a writhing grey, squirming and pulsating with whatever maggots and larvae had made a home in its tissues. Some of the packaging, too, had begun to break down, the juices within them hardened to putrid, crusting puddles of blackened blood on the surface of the counter. The stench of it all twisted Susan's stomach into knots; seemed to cling to the hairs in her nostrils.

Eventually, when she could take no more of it, she flung open the back door – flooding the room with the fresh, cleansing air of the garden outside.

This has to stop, she thought, and reached for her phone. *Enough is enough.*

CHAPTER 18

1955

D r. Baker's behaviour had grown even more unpredictable since Olivia's death. He'd significantly upped his daily dosage of pills, Grace had noticed – forever popping them from the bottle he kept in his jacket pocket – and he looked permanently dishevelled, which for him was *very* odd indeed: he prided himself on being immaculate. The atmosphere in the house was frayed and it was clear to Grace that things were starting to disintegrate. Father Jameson was drinking more, was less steady on his feet; even Sister Tabby seemed drained, a woman questioning her life choices.

Sinead, as she was the only one Baker was currently medicating, was now of greatest concern to the rest of the girls. Ruth, who shared a bedroom with her, had observed she wasn't sleeping at night, which left her tired during the days, and both Grace and Ellen could see how bewildered she was, how withdrawn and depressed – more so even than she'd been when she'd first arrived at Montpellier Street. One morning, Grace had caught her rocking back and forth in the rocking chair in her bedroom, humming a lullaby and cradling *something* – but when Grace had approached her, she'd seen Sinead's arms were empty.

On good days, Sinead only sang to her phantom child; on bad days, she'd bang her head against the walls and fidget with the chain around her neck so aggressively the pads of her finger would bleed... though she cried bloody murder when Sister Tabby tried to take the chain away from her. It had been a gift from her mother, apparently, and she wore it to keep herself safe – though Grace couldn't understand why Sinead was so attached to something given to her by a woman who'd thrown her away when she'd needed her most.

Ellen had been subdued since the night they'd found Olivia's body. Grace had stayed by the bathroom door to try and protect her from it all: the blood, the mirror – the one reflecting the other back on itself, a crimson mirror ball. That had been the plan. But then the Doctor had arrived on the scene, had flung the door wide open and revealed all... and Grace could no longer protect Ellen from the horror. Any of it.

With the bathroom in its entirety exposed, she'd seen the white walls, sprayed with jets and gushes of arterial blood from Olivia's neck. The blood had still been pulsing from her body, her heart still beating, unaware of the futility of its efforts – the spurts racing each one another down the wall, reminding Grace of a game she'd played with her younger brother on the rainy days they'd sat indoors, watching raindrops track down the window and guessing which would reach the windowsill below first. She'd snapped quickly out of the reverie – but not before she'd been assailed by a flash of her brother's face, forever frozen in time, eaten up by the fire that meant he'd never age, never grow.

Baker had ushered them out onto the landing and ordered them into their bedroom. Grace had taken Ellen's hand as they'd walked away, turning back around just long enough to catch sight of the Doctor standing frozen in the doorway, panic darting across his normally calm face: his hands in his hair, the very picture of despair.

He's losing it, Grace had thought to herself. Then had followed Ellen into the bedroom and quietly closed the door.

Ellen was handing sheets to Grace. They'd been handwashed; would need to go out onto the washing line in the back garden. The sun was shining, but there was a strong wind – it was, as Grace's mother would have said, *a fine day for drying clothes.*

"Are you okay?" Grace said.

Ellen seemed taken aback that Grace would ask so stupid a question, but answered her anyway. "I suppose so. I mean, we have to be, don't we?"

"We don't *have* to be anything." Grace stepped closer to Ellen and put a hand on her shoulder. "What we saw... it was awful, just awful and we can't ever unsee it. But we can talk about it, be there for each other."

"I don't want to talk about it, Grace. I want to forget about it. Olivia is gone, Baker is... God knows what—not a real doctor, anyway—and Father Jameson isn't even pretending to hold it together anymore."

"We need to get out of here," Grace said. "Me, you and Ruth. Get out and then get help for Sinead."

"Grab the sheets," Ellen said, opening the back door, "and let's get these hung out."

"Did you hear me? We need to get out of here before things get worse."

Ellen turned back around, looking her right in the eye. "I heard you, but we can't talk in the house. Come on, grab the sheets."

It was a beautiful, fresh day and as stifled as the girls had felt indoors, being outside gave them at least the temporary sense that things were... normal. Manageable.

By the washing line, the crisp white bed linen in her hand, Ellen tilted her face up to the sun, drinking it in. Grace stared at her and smiled; moments like this, with Ellen – mundane as they were – were her favourite.

Once the washing was hung out, they sat cross-legged in the grass, feeling the sun warm their limbs, their fingers busy making daisy chains. It felt odd to relax, wrong, given their current predicament – but right then, they were free, somewhere far away from Montpellier Street. Though it couldn't last, Grace knew; they'd have to go inside soon enough. It was almost lunchtime, and they had food to prepare for the others. Ruth was resting in bed more and more these days, her belly getting bigger and bigger as her due date neared, and Sister Tabby had gone into town to get supplies.

Where the men of the house were, Grace had no idea – and hoped to remain in the dark for as long as possible.

Ellen stood up first and stretched her arms to the sky. "Is Sister Tabby back already?" she said, pointing to a figure in the window above them. "I didn't hear the car."

Grace followed Ellen's line of sight upwards. "I don't think that's Tabby." She lifted her hand to shield her eyes from the sun. "It's Sinead."

"So it is." Ellen paused, apparently considering something. When she spoke again, she was audibly anxious. "Oh God, what's she doing in the Sister's bedroom? She knows that's off limits. We need to run up there and get her out before someone else sees her."

They hurried inside and up the stairs. Around them, the house was still; eerily quiet. Father Jameson's study door was closed, but his coat was there on the stand in the hall, Grace saw; probably, she thought, he'd fallen asleep at his desk again. The door to Sister Tabby's bedroom *was* open, however, and Grace let herself in, lightly knocking as she entered. Ellen stayed by the open door.

"Sinead?" she asked, trying to keep her voice level. "What are you doing in here? Are you okay?" Sinead was still standing by the window, facing outside, her back to them.

Sinead responded but didn't turn around. "I'm fine, thank you. It's such a beautiful day. The sun, it's...quite beautiful."

"Why don't you come with us and we'll go outside?" said Ellen from the doorway.

"It's okay," Sinead told her, continuing to stare through the window at the garden below. "I can see her from here. I have my eye on her."

A sick feeling was building in the pit of Grace's stomach, a foreboding that was becoming increasingly familiar. She wanted to walk out of the room: to sprint down the stairs and through the front door. She wanted to take Ellen by the hand and lead her away from Montpellier Street forever, but she knew she couldn't. Instead, she asked the question, the one she was absolutely sure she didn't want to hear Sinead answer.

"*Who* can you see? Who's in the garden?"

"Elenore," Sinead said, matter-of-factly, turning finally to look at Grace. "My daughter. She loves playing outside."

The sick feeling spread and bloomed, turning Grace's insides to water.

"Sinead," she told her, "your daughter doesn't live here. She's..."

"We should go down and see her," Ellen said.

Grace glanced at Ellen, confused – but Ellen was smiling at Sinead. Her warm face would put anyone at ease, Grace thought. And remembered their mission: getting Sinead out of the room before anyone got home and she got into trouble. Now, perhaps, was not the time to unravel her hallucinations.

A scrape of wood and a high-pitched screech interrupted her, mid-thought. She spun back around to Sinead, and saw the large sash window was now open, the glass pushed all the way up to the top of the frame, and Sinead now leaning out of it, the palms of both hands resting on the ledge as she watched her ghost-child play in the garden beyond.

"Don't lean out like that – please." Grace took a half step forward, until she was halfway between Sinead and Ellen. "It's windy out. You need to be careful."

Sinead removed her hands from the ledge. "Such a fresh day," she said, smiling. "I love this weather – bright and sunny, not too warm." She leaned back against the windowsill and lifted herself up onto it, letting her legs dangling into the room. The smile was broad, sincere, lighting up the whole of her face. Grace had never once seen her look that way before, not in all the time she'd been in the house. She seemed... peaceful. Genuinely happy.

Whatever medication they've got her on, Grace thought, *it's made her forget where she is. Even if it has made her hallucinate.*

"This is my favourite type of weather, too," Grace said, relaxing into what might have been the most normal conversation she'd ever had with her housemate. "I love going on long walks when it's like this; everything's so refreshing."

Sinead, still smiling, pulled her legs up onto the windowsill and pressed her back against the frame. Half in, half out of the window.

"I named her after my grandmother, Elenore," she said. "Granny Nor, we called her." Sinead closed her eyes, remembering. "She used to take us down the backroads to pick blackberries, bring us home after to make jam. Her kitchen always smelled of baking. She made the best tarts."

"That's nice. A lovely name, it is." Ellen took a long step inside the room; she spoke softly, the words falling on Grace like a warm blanket.

A change came over Sinead's face, a darkness. Grace saw it happen; saw the realisation of where she was bringing Sinead back, painfully, into the room, into the reality of her life as it really was. The contrast reminded Grace of how bright blue crashing waves sometimes had masses of dark seaweed churning inside them – hiding in plain sight, just below the surface.

"They never even let me hold her," Sinead said. "Not once, not even for a second. I begged them, I *begged* them to let me see her, but they wouldn't." The smile had slipped from Sinead's face.

Ellen took another step into the room. "Sinead, it's going to be okay," she said, her tone still low and gentle. "It is."

Sinead hugged her knees into her chest and squeezed her eyes shut, tears now welling in the corners. "They made me give her up. They made me." She blinked twice; craned her neck and looked right at them. "They made me write a different name on the papers... someone else's name, not mine." She looked back up, into the sun. "They made me," she repeated.

"You'll find her, you will," Ellen said. "Or she'll find you."

"No. She won't."

The words were cold, hard; the voice so unlike Sinead's they might have come from someone else's mouth. They were the last thing Grace heard before Sinead dipped her left shoulder and let herself roll out of the window.

It was Ellen's face Grace fixed on then, the slow opening of her mouth and widening of her eyes in horror as she lunged forward to the place where Sinead had been, struggling for something she'd never reach. Time slowed to a crawl. And then Sinead was gone, and there was nothing. Where she'd been was just an empty, open window – like some kind of grotesque magic trick.

Grace would never forget the sounds, though: the brief, soft fluttering of Sinead's nightdress on the wind, and thereafter the dull, dense thud of a body hitting a pavement, a head cracking open on concrete steps. They confirmed what she'd already known: that there was no need to rush outside, no need to call for help.

And then Grace was on her knees, and Ellen was screaming.

E ventually, Grace picked herself up off the bedroom floor and walked to the windowsill; pulled Ellen away from it, but didn't look down.

She couldn't have said how long they held each other in that room, Ellen sobbing loudly into her shoulder, Grace holding her up when Ellen's knees gave way. Only that they stopped when Grace heard the car pulling into the drive: Sister Tabby, most likely, or Baker. And while she didn't care about Baker, she didn't want Tabby to stumble onto the scene in the backyard alone.

"We need to go downstairs," she told Ellen.

They made their way out of the room, Ellen's hand shaking in hers, Ellen's body beginning to show signs of shock; she looked white as a ghost. They passed the priest's study, but the door was still closed, the rest of the house still quiet as the grave. Whoever had arrived back, they weren't inside yet.

"Go out front and tell whoever is out there what happened," Grace said, at the bottom of the stairs. "I'll meet you out the back."

She made for the kitchen, through the little back scullery where they did the laundry. Her legs felt like they were pushing against water, her body physically resisting going into the garden. At the back door she paused and took a deep breath before pulling open the door and stepping out.

In the middle of the garden, the sheets were billowing, blinding white, in the wind – but were spattered now with blood, vivid red streaked across them like brush strokes on rippling canvas. It took all the strength she had to walk over to the body; she hadn't looked out of the window, when they'd been upstairs, but the height, the sound, the sheets... she had a sense already of what she'd find. She just hoped she was prepared to see it.

She wasn't.

Sinead's nightdress was red now, too: deep red, saturated. She'd fallen on her back, face up; her head had split open on the concrete, but her face – except for a light misting of blood – looked much the same as it had. She looked calm, still.

She hadn't screamed when it happened, Grace remembered.

There was more blood around the body, a growing pool of it. But Sinead's chain, she saw, was still around her neck, albeit matted with gore – the silver edges of the St. Brigid's cross glistening in the sunlight. The marble had been damaged in the fall, and a small crack ran through its centre.

It wasn't broken, though, Grace realised. Only fractured.

CHAPTER 19

2018

"Your neighbour called me. Susan?" Louise said, in lieu of any more formal *hello*.

Nicole's mouth fell open. All the missed phone calls, all those unreturned messages... and finally her sister had given up waiting. Which was why she was now standing on Nicole's doorstep, demanding answers.

"Were you just going to ignore me forever?" she added.

"I was going to call you," Nicole said. It was a lie, and an obvious one at that.

"How have you been?" Louise's voice softened; she'd never been able to stay mad at her younger sister for long. "I missed you. Are you going to let me in?"

"The house is in... a bit of a state, still."

"Yes, so I heard – as I said, Susan called. What's going on, Nick?"

To Nicole's horror, Louise didn't wait for an answer – just barged past her and into the hallway.

"No – wait! Please...wait." Nicole felt a blinding pain in her head, something like a migraine – an epic one – sweeping through her brain. She stopped still and dug her fingers into her temples, trying for some semblance of relief.

"Are you okay?" Louise asked her, alarmed. "Nick, can you hear me? Are you okay?"

"Yes." Nicole held up a hand, forestalling further questions. "I'm okay. It's a headache – just a blinding headache."

"Do you have painkillers?"

"Yeah. In the drawer in the sitting room – Jess put them there, I think."

Louise took a step back, her forehead knitting in confusion, disbelief.

"What?" Nicole asked her, still rubbing at her temples. "What did I say?"

Seven Months Earlier

Nicole was in the kitchen unpacking the groceries when she felt Jessica come up behind her, wrap her arms around Nicole's waist and lean into her back.

"Hi," she mumbled, from somewhere in Nicole's shoulders.

"Hi," Nicole said. Then: "How am I so lucky, that I get to have you?"

"I don't know, but I'm yours now." Jessica rose up on her tiptoes and kissed the back of Nicole's neck, before pulling away; walked across to one of the shopping bags and began to root around in it. "I'm going to start dinner. Where's the mince?"

"Are you sure it's not there?" Nicole craned her neck to peer into the open bag. "I could have sworn I picked it up."

"Nope. Definitely not in here."

"Crap. Okay, I'll go back, it won't take long." Nicole snatched up the keys and headed for the door. "I'll be right back. It's worth going to get it – we can't have spaghetti Bolognese without mince."

"Fine," Jess said. "But I'm coming too. It's our first night in this house and I don't want to be alone. And I know you: you'll spend ages in the shop and end up coming back with everything but the mince."

"You have no faith in me." Nicole reached forward and grabbed Jess, pulling her into her. "I love you."

"Good, I love you too." Jess reached up and kissed Nicole gently on the lips. "Now, are we going? I'm starving."

"Wake up! Can you hear me? Wake up!"

The ringing in Nicole's ears was unbearable – high-pitched and unrelenting. She brought her hands up to her head, trying to somehow crush the sound out of her own skull, but there was no escaping it.

"Jess? Baby, can you hear me? Wake up!"

The smell nauseated her: the burning, the smoke. It was all around her now, distorting her vision. Though there was a stillness there too, somehow; a silence.

She couldn't move her head, not much, but she let her eyes scan her surroundings. She needed some sense of where she was; of what had happened.

She was in the car, she saw. Still in the car. But everything was wrong. The seat belt, cutting into her chest, slicing at the flesh there; the ringing, hard and painful in her ears.

The smoke was beginning to subside. But the burning smell remained, stinging her eyes and invading her nostrils. The pain in her chest was spreading, shooting down her arms in pulsing waves; there was acid in her throat. She closed her eyes to steady herself.

When she opened them again, she saw Jess. Somehow, impossibly, below her.

How can she be there?

The car. The car is on its side.

She took stock of her surroundings. Now the smoke was clearing, she could see out of the windscreen, shattered though it was. The world was sideways; she, Nicole, was hanging from her seat with nothing but her seatbelt holding her in place, protecting her from gravity. Another stab of pain shot through her head; she touched her temple and felt something hot and sticky and liquid there, flowing from the gouges in her skin.

Blood.

She could smell it now, taste it, like copper in her mouth. Blood, and powder: the fine talc-like particles of the powder that seemed to be settling on every surface of the car's interior.

Jessica hadn't moved, not once.

Blood dropped from Nicole's arm – dripped down, landing softly on Jessica's face. But she didn't stir. Her eyes were open, yes – but unfocused. Pale and empty and clouded over, the eyes of another person altogether.

Nicole felt her own eyes closing, her head heavy. She willed herself to stay awake, but couldn't do it, couldn't keep herself conscious. She was drifting. One last time, she called out to Jessica, but the words came out a tired whisper, and her voice broke around them.

"Please, Jess. Please, wake up."

L ouise touched her arm, and Nicole flinched at the contact.

"It's just me," Louise said. "You're okay." Her voice was deliberately soothing, but strained. She was choking back tears, Nicole thought.

Louise was trying to stay calm, she could tell. Was trying to make it seem normal, make it manageable; make it appear as if there was nothing for Nicole to worry about, as if denying your wife had died and carrying on as before was perfectly ordinary, thoroughly unremarkable. Just a blip; just part of the grieving process.

Denial was one of the five stages, after all.

Finally, she met Louise's eye. "You think I've lost my mind." Her voice was devoid of emotion; devoid of just about everything.

"No, Nicky. No. I just think... maybe you're hurting more than we knew."

"*Nicky*? It must be worse than I thought – you never call me that." She was trying for levity, but couldn't maintain it. Nothing about this situation was sustainable. "This *is* bad, isn't it Lou?" she added, sounding small and broken.

"Yeah. This is bad." Louise reached out and pulled her into a tight embrace. "But I'm here now. I've got you."

They stood like that, in the hall, for a very long time.

"You're awake."

The bright light was scorching, blinding. She closed her eyes against them, but not before she'd caught the outline of a figure beside her bed.

"Jessica?"

"No, it's me." Louise leaned forward in the bedside chair she'd been occupying and took Nicole's hand. "How are you feeling?"

"What happened?" Nicole forced her eyes to stay open; forced them to focus on her sister. "The car, it was... on its side. Jessica was knocked out. Where is she?"

Louise leaned back and ran a hand over her face, then rose halfway to standing and shifted position, until she was sitting at the edge of the bed. "Nicky, I'm so sorry. Jess is gone. She... She's gone." She spoke gently, as if the news would hurt less, the more softly she said it.

Nicole listened without understanding, the words impossible to hear, to make sense of.

"But she was just there. We were just talking. What happened?" She'd begun to cry, though it barely registered. The pain in her chest was back, the burning.

"I'm so sorry." Louise was crying now, too. "She just never woke up."

CHAPTER 20

1955

T he back door swung open, snapping Grace out of her trance. She looked down at her feet and saw the blood, Sinead's blood, had spread, had reached her shoes. Somewhere in her peripheral vision, the ruined bed linen still flickered in the breeze.

There were panicked voices all around her – and then screaming, not high pitched but guttural. Ellen was beside her, guiding Ruth gently to the ground after trying but failing to hold her upright; Ruth was sobbing, weeping into her cupped hands.

Doctor Baker was there, too; returned, apparently, from wherever he'd been.

"No," he was whispering, raking his fingers across his scalp. "This can't be happening." Then, more loudly, aggressively: "Why? *Why* is this happening?"

Grace started, frightened by his outburst. He looked now, she thought, much as he had the night they'd found Olivia: a man undone, tearing at his own hair, panic crackling like electricity across his features.

"What's wrong with you?" he shouted, at no one in particular. "Why are you all so fucking *weak*?"

She edged away from him, doing her best to insert herself between him and the other girls still huddled together on the grass.

"Don't you see?" He was still talking, still raging, livid now, the vein in his forehead bulging, his face reddening. "I'm trying to help you people, to *fix* you! But your tiny, pathetic minds just... snap, don't they? They just *snap*."

"That's enough!" The force of her own response shocked even Grace. "You need to call someone, have them take Sinead away. And *we* need to go back to the main house with everyone else." She gestured to Ruth and Ellen behind her. "And you can yell all you want, but we know about you. We know you're not a doctor anymore."

Baker's hands fell to his sides. "What did you say to me?"

Grace walked backwards until she felt her foot strike Ellen's. "Get up," she told her, not looking back. "Help Ruth and start moving inside." She looked back to Baker, then added, loudly: "We're leaving now, *Mr* Baker. We're going to go inside, and then we're leaving."

Ruth and Ellen got to their feet and began walking as quickly as Ruth's condition would allow them towards the house. Grace – her eyes still on Baker – followed.

He looked defeated, she thought. Or perhaps she simply hoped this was the case.

"Where will we go?" Ellen asked, when they reached the kitchen.

"We just need to get out the front door and through the gate," Grace said. "There'll be someone on the street. We'll get help somewhere."

Ruth was still in the nightdress she'd been wearing while she napped. She had a hand over her stomach, as always, but her breathing seemed off, to Grace; more laboured than it should have been.

"Get a coat on, Ruth," she told her, pulling her own coat from the back of the kitchen door. "We need to hurry."

"I can't move fast. Something feels...wrong," Ruth said, undeniably breathless now.

Ellen put an arm under her for support. "Come on," she said. "Please, we have to go now."

"The baby's in some distress," Baker said, from the doorway. "I wouldn't be rushing off anywhere in that condition, Ruth." Something had changed in him, Grace thought; he didn't look defeated anymore. No; he looked deranged. "In truth, of course, I can't let any of you go. I think perhaps you know that."

He spoke gently now, kindly and softly, the calmness somehow more disquieting even than his outburst in the garden.

Grace drew her shoulders back. "Look here…" she began.

"No, *you* look here!" The volume of his voice made all three of them jump. "You don't just walk out of here without permission. You have been placed in my care, all of you. I *own* you. And more than that: I can *help* you. Grace – I can cure you of your affliction. Surely you'd like that?"

Grace furrowed her brow, confused. "My *affliction*?"

"Yes, child. Your affliction. You think we don't see the way you look at Ellen, the way you touch her? We know what you are, all of us. Don't you want to be normal?"

Grace felt her cheeks redden.

"And Ruth," he continued. "Let's be realistic. You can't possibly look after that baby, can you? Whereas *I* – I already have parents ready to raise it, love it. To give it the life you'll never be able to."

Ruth stiffened. "*Take* my baby? What are you talking about? I would *never* let you have my child. Jesus Christ, you have lost your mind? Come on, girls," she added, to Grace and Ellen. "We're leaving, right now."

"Stop." Baker stepped forward into the room. There was a knife in his hand: a butcher's knife, the same one Grace had washed so many times in the kitchen sink. He'd taken it from the draining board, she realised, though she hadn't seen him do it.

He was quick, she'd say that for him. Quick, and cunning.

"I don't care to repeat myself," he said, "but I reiterate: none of you are leaving this house. I can't let that happen. Are you understanding me? What happened in England... I'm not about to let it happen here. I will not. It may be that I'm surrounded by narrow-minded idiots wherever I go, that no one is prepared to see what I'm trying to do or the strides I'm trying to make in medicine – that nobody is willing to take the necessary risks. But I must stand firm, don't you see? *We* must, you and I. We must test, if we're to progress."

"And taking people's babies away?" Ruth spat at him – her hand still protecting her stomach. "How does that fit with your medical advances?"

He shrugged, dismissive – as if what she'd said was an irrelevance and Ruth herself an afterthought. "There are people out there who want to be parents, but can't. And they're willing to *pay* for the privilege of looking after your bastard Irish children – pay a great deal of money. You should be happy they're willing to. There'd be no means of subsidising any of your treatments without them."

We need to let him talk, Grace thought. *Let him rant and rave as long as it takes for Sister Tabby to come back to the house and...*

Except, she remembered, there was someone else in the house already, besides them and the Doctor. Father Jameson's coat was hanging up in the hallway, she'd seen it – which meant the priest was likely in his office. That *he* could help them, right now.

The question was: should she risk antagonising Baker by calling for a priest who might not even wake up from his drunken nap?

Baker walked towards them, the knife in his hand extending out from his body. "Enough of this," he said. "I need to handle that... incident outside, and I need you out of my hair to do it." He touched his bottom lip with the tip of his knife, weighing up his options. "To the basement. I think. Yes: that would be best, for now."

There'd be no escaping the basement once they were down there; Grace knew that well enough by now. She couldn't let him take them there.

She had to stall.

"So you can *handle* it?" she said.

"What?" Baker seemed to be growing agitated again.

"You said you had to *handle the incident outside*. What do you mean by that? Are you going to call the undertaker? Sister Fitzgerald?"

Baker hesitated. "I'll be dealing with Sinead myself," he said after a moment "I can't risk having that much attention on my work here. Other people... get in the way. It was hard enough to explain away Belle and what happened to her eyes. No: one body was enough. More than enough."

"Two," Grace corrected him. "Olivia needed *explaining away*, too."

"Olivia?" He paused a second time – a tiny, self-satisfied smile playing at the corners of his mouth. "No. We... didn't involve any outside parties, in that instance."

"What did you do with her?" This was Ruth again, her rage now palpable.

"She's... around. Now," Baker gestured down at the knife, "shall we adjourn to the basement, so we can get ourselves cleaned up?"

He herded them into the hall, the knife barely inches from the small of Grace's back. Ruth, she was acutely aware, was in no state to run. But nor could Grace let her – or, God forbid, Ellen – be put in that basement.

She had to do something. Now.

She began to scream, at the top of her lungs.

"FATHER JAMESON!!! FATHER—"

"Don't bother," Baker cut in. "He'll be asleep. And at any rate, do you really expect *him* to intervene?" The smile widened, contorting the lower reaches of his face. "Who do you think's been facilitating the adoptions, for heaven's sake? Jameson and Fitzgerald have been shipping babies off to England and America for *years* – and let's just say, they're not doing it out of the goodness of their hearts." He marched them just past the basement door, unlocked it and ushered them through. "Go inside."

The girls didn't move: Grace still holding out for Sister Tabby to walk through the front door, or a sober Father Jameson to hear them and come to his senses.

The knife twitched in Baker's hands – then, before Grace could blink, much less do anything to intercede, was pressed against the soft skin at Ellen's throat.

"You first, Grace," he said, looking directly at her as he spoke. "Down you go – there's a good girl."

Her movements were automatic, involuntary; it was, she'd think later, as if someone else altogether was controlling her body as it descended the stairs. She could think only of Ellen; of the knife, and the pinpricks of blood already rising at the point where the tip of the blade met her neck.

And then there was darkness: nothing but darkness, all around her.

The first thing she saw, when she came back to herself, was Ruth – doubled over in pain, both hands clutched to her stomach and Ellen rubbing her back. But for the three of them and Baker's torture-table, the basement was empty.

"What are we going to do?" Ellen asked.

But Grace had nothing to offer her; not a single, solitary answer. "I don't know," she said. "I don't know."

There was no way out of the room. And even if they *did* get out, they'd still be in the house, wouldn't they? Or, if they somehow managed to escape the house... where would they go? They had nowhere; no-one.

She sunk to the ground, utterly defeated.

"What do you mean you don't know?" Ellen said, as angry as Grace as ever heard her.

"I mean, we're trapped. I don't know what to do."

"Can you both...please...stop?" said Ruth, her breath coming in slow, strained gasps.

Grace took a breath of her own.

"Okay," she said. "I'm sorry. I'm sorry. We just... need to think. *I* need to think. I've been stuck in here before, that's all, and I know after that that the only way out is through the main door. The best we can do – the *only* thing we can do – is go up there and get ready to rush whoever opens the door next."

"What about ...that?" Ruth pointed up at the window.

"It doesn't open," Grace told her. "It's just a pane of glass."

"So break it," Ellen said, without hesitation. "Who are we worried about upsetting?"

Ruth and Grace shared a glance.

"How?" Grace asked, already looking around them for a suitable object. The room, she saw, was as barren as it had been the last time she'd been down there. There was nothing they could use to smash the glass, nothing but...

The mop.

Wordlessly, the other two girls staring after her, she raced to the top of the stairs grabbed the mop from its bucket, and sprinted down again.

"This," she said, holding it aloft.

There was a loud crash from above. Grace flinched; Ruth instinctively placed a hand over her bump. Ellen ran up to the top of the stairs and pressed an ear against the door.

"They're arguing," she said, dropping to a whisper.

Grace joined her at the top of the stairs, and listened. Father Jameson and Baker were fighting, from the sounds of it: it was muffled, difficult to make out every word, but it was clear enough to Grace that Father Jameson had stumbled across Baker cleaning up the back garden.

"I can't get involved," the priest was saying in his customary drunken slur. "I won't. Not again..."

Baker was easier to understand, not least because he was shouting.

"You will do exactly what I tell you," he told Jameson. "You think people finding out you've been stealing from the church is bad? Wait until I tell them you've been selling babies to pay for your...habits. We're in this together now, Alan. We need to figure out what to do with the other three – but first, we need to hose down the back garden."

"They're going outside," Ellen said. "We need to go, now."

Grace grabbed the mop, and the two of them retreated back into to the basement, re-joining Ruth by the window.

"What did you hear?" Ruth asked them. "I could just hear two people shouting. Is Father Jameson coming down?" Her breathing had settled down again, Grace noticed.

"No one is coming," Grace said. She struck the glass with the handle of the mop, poking a fist-sized hole in the glass.

She jabbed at it again, then again, a little of the glass coming away and tinkling to the ground each time until there was nothing but fresh air in the frame. The window was so small, she realised, she'd had to remove every inch of glass to create a space large enough for them to crawl through.

For her and Ellen to crawl through, anyway. Ruth, it was dawning on her, would never be able to fit through the gap – not with her belly so swollen.

"Is there any way you can get out?" Grace asked her – still looking up at the empty window frame, afraid to look the pregnant woman in the eye.

"Definitely not. But you two go and get help, okay?" Ruth put her hand on Grace's arm and pulled her into a hug. "Just... don't forget about me."

Grace was crying now, silently; couldn't help it. The tears left tracks down the sides of her nose; she wiped them away on Ruth's shoulder. "We'll come right back for you," she said. Then: "Ellen, get over here." She beckoned to Ellen, not turning around. "I'll give you a boost up. Step into my hands."

"Wait, she'll cut herself," Ruth said, concerned. "Here – hang on." She shucked off her coat, unbuttoned the cardigan underneath, and handed them both to Ellen. "Put these along the frame. They'll protect from the jagged bits."

Ellen put her arms around Ruth and squeezed. "Thank you, she said. "And you are coming out right after me?" she added to Grace, slowly untangling herself from Ruth.

"Right after you," Grace said. "But look – you need to go around to the front and crouch down, as soon as you're out. You can't risk anyone in the back garden seeing you. Understand?"

"I understand. Just... please don't take too long, okay?" Ellen put her arms around Grace, now. "And so you know," she said, so quietly only Grace could hear her, "I like the way you look at me."

Ellen kissed her – just once, on the cheek – and Grace smiled. "Step into my hands," she said.

She laced her fingers together, creating a hammock shape with both hands, and waited. Ellen climbed onto her hands, left foot first, and Grace lifted her up to the window.

Above, them, the door opened – then slammed immediately closed again, as whoever had walked through it shut it behind them. The three of them froze where they stood, Grace struggling to hold Ellen in place at the window frame.

She heard cursing; footsteps, making their way down the stairs.

"Where is it?" Baker was shouting, getting louder with every thud of his feet on the staircase. "The mop is always by the box of bleach. Where is it? What did you do with it?"

Ruth's eyes darted to the mop, propped up now against the basement wall.

Too late.

Baker really *was* quick: he'd made it already to the bottom step. In the gloom of the basement, he looked to Grace like something out of a nightmare. His suit jacket was off, though he still wore his blood-splattered dress shirt. Blood was matted into the dark hair on his forearms; his pupils were blown wide, deranged, and his lips were curled into an expression of pure fury. The knife from the kitchen was still in his hands.

Is that Sinead's blood, Grace couldn't stop herself wondering – *or Father Jameson's?*

Or Sister Tabby? Oh, God – Sister Tabby...

His mad eyes widened further as he took in the scene before him.

"Ellen go, just go!" Grace shouted, before he could speak – pushing upwards with all her might, and launching Ellen through the opening in the frame.

Ellen was scrambling, half in and half out of the window. She placed the palms of her hands on the wall outside and pushed against it, doing all she could to force herself through. Her legs were still dangling into the room when Baker came rushing at Grace and Ruth – charging them like a wounded bull.

"Get back here!" he shouted.

Ruth grabbed the mop and brought the handle down on his wrist. The knife flew from his hand, and he roared – in pain or anger, Grace couldn't tell. The knife handle bounced off his shoe and flew into the far corner of the room.

Ruth brought the mop down on him again, making contact with the side of his head –the force she used so great that the handle snapped in two on impact. He put his hand to his head and fell forwards, stumbling onto his knees.

Ruth threw the other piece of the handle at him and turned to Grace, her own fingers locked together. "Go, now," she said. "Come on, into my hands."

Grace hesitated, her rising panic freezing her to the stop. "Ellen," she shouted through the window. "Run and get help, now."

"I don't want to leave you," Ellen shouted back from outside.

"Go on," Ruth said, one palm on Grace's shoulder, "get yourself out. I'll be okay."

She proffered her hands, and Grace stepped into them, just as Ellen reached a hand back through the window and pulled her up and out. She wiggled through the frame, feeling the little shards of glass cut into her stomach.

She twisted her neck around, intending to reassure Ruth they'd be back, that she'd be safe, and saw Baker, back on his feet and standing directly behind Ruth, blood-soaked and monstrous – one end of the broken mop handle gripped like a stake in his hand. Time slowed, and Grace felt her own heart pounding in her ears, drowning out whatever Ellen was saying outside. She tried to call out to Ruth, to warn her, but her throat was tightening, seizing.

And Baker was raising the handle and plunging it, hard, into the back of Ruth's neck.

Shock, then disbelief and finally terror spread like an oil slick across the pregnant girl's face. Then Ellen was screaming, and an awful gurgling sound was rising from Ruth's mouth, bright blood cascading out of it as she struggled for breath. Such was the force of the strike that the splintered handle had skewered her, piercing her from neck to throat. Her hands clawed at the ragged wood protruding from her windpipe, but it was hopeless.

Grace looked back at her in horror. It took her longer than it should have to notice that Baker was no longer in the basement.

"Run," she told Ellen. "We need to run, now."

The last thing she saw before she left Montpellier Street for good was Ruth, swaying on her feet, her knees beginning to give way. And then Ellen was grabbing her arm, pulling her to her feet, and they were running, running – somewhere else, somewhere far from there.

CHAPTER 21

2018

"Nick?" Louise said, taking her sister's hand. "Nick, you have to stop running from this."

"I'm here," Nicole told her. Then: "I'm sorry."

Her voice was weak; breaking around the edges. She let Louise's hand fall from hers and took a few steps away, wrapping her arms around her own body for comfort.

Louise surveyed the room: taking in the dishes piled up in and all around the sink, the overflowing bin by the door. There were tins of food everywhere, open and discarded; some half-eaten, the other half left to rot and moulder. How could Nick live like this, in this squalor? She cursed herself for not coming sooner. She was supposed to be a bloody psychiatrist, wasn't she? She should have seen the signs.

"I'm sorry," she told Louise.

"Why are you apologising?" Nicole ran a hand through her hair. "I'm the fuck-up. I'm the one you have to come and help, again."

"You're my sister, and you're not a fuck up – you're grieving. Jess died, and you're hurting. Susan... she was only worried about you, that's all. Just worried."

Nicole took her head in her hands. "Oh, God. She thinks I'm crazy, doesn't she? Talking to my wife who isn't there. Jesus."

"She doesn't think you're crazy. She just knew you needed some support. That's why she called me, to find out what happened and tell me that you needed me."

Nicole took a deep breath and closed her eyes. "I just couldn't do it."

"Do what?" Louise's voice was gentle, understanding.

"Be without her. I don't want to do any of this without her." She opened her eyes again. "I can't go to the places we used to go; stand where she used to stand. It's like she's everywhere and nowhere at the same time."

Louise didn't speak. Just listened, the way she should have insisted on doing weeks ago.

"It started off just... imagining her reactions to things, you know? Thinking of what she might say about a TV show or a neighbour who kept calling around. And then she was... here, next to me – when I woke up in the mornings, when I fell asleep at night. Standing behind me when I was making dinner. She was just...back. I brought her back to me."

Nicole's voice broke. She was crying, now. "She was the only person I needed. And it's not fair, Lou. It's not fair that she's gone. This was meant to be *our* kitchen, *our* house. This was supposed to be our *life*. This was all we wanted, and I don't want it without her."

"Nick," Louise crossed the floor and enveloped her in a hug, "it's going to get better. It is. You can do this, I know you can. We'll do it together, okay?"

Nicole looked up at her. "Okay," she said. "Okay." She wasn't sure she believed Louise, believed any of the things she was promising. But she wanted to, so badly.

The doorbell rang.

"Susan," they said in unison.

"You wanna meet her in person?" Nicole asked, sniffling and wiping her face with the back of her hand.

"Yeah, I'd like to meet her, I think. Are you okay with that, though? With her being here?"

Nicole felt her cheeks burn; remembered all the times she'd spoken about Jess in front of Susan, spoken *to* Jess in front of her, and dreaded what the older woman must have thought of her.

"I have to face her again some time, I guess," she said finally, and made for the hallway.

Susan was, of course, at the door when she opened it: standing on the top step with a plate in her hand and a tea towel hanging over it, to protect whatever was hidden underneath.

"Well, now," she said, "I saw your sister arrived, so I thought I better bring around some scones." She breezed past Nicole and headed straight to the kitchen. "Well, hello," Nicole heard her boom, when she got there. "You must be Louise..."

Nicole smiled to herself; she should have known Susan wouldn't make a fuss, would carry on as normal. There was no need to make someone who was feeling bad feel worse, and Susan would know that. Nicole loved that about her.

After tea and scones, the three of them had set to cleaning the house. There was no real discussion about the task; rather, it seemed to happen organically, a natural extension of their conversation. That was Louise and Susan's doing, Nicole knew – and she was grateful for it, thankful to have in her life the kind of women who would pick her up and carry without judgement or interrogation.

She mopped the floor. It was gentle work; meditative.

When the time came to dispose of the water from the mop bucket outside, she found Susan sitting on the back step, staring out into the garden.

"Having a break?" Nicole asked, wandering over to her.

"Oh – yes, love. It's the cleaning fumes – they make me a bit lightheaded. Thought I could do with the air." Susan looked up at her and patted the step; Nicole took the hint and sat down next to her. "And how are you feeling, love? Nice to see your sister?"

"Look, Susan," Nicole started, "I'm so, so sor—"

"Ah, don't you start apologising," Susan said, not letting her finish. "It's not just ghosts, you know, that get stuck reliving things that hurt them. The living do it, too; it's a strange compulsion we have, to hurt ourselves with memories. But the difference between you and the ghosts is that *you didn't die*, love. You're still here, and you have to keep going; you can't be haunting yourself."

"I know, I do. I'm going to try and pull myself together. Get on with it."

Susan shook her head. "That might be where you're going wrong. It's *supposed* to hurt, grief, isn't it? Too many people try to avoid it, try to dodge the pain. But I think the trick is to let yourself feel it – feel it all, but know it won't last forever."

"Maybe you're right." Nicole got up and dusted off her jeans. "I should go back in. But... thank you. For everything. I'm not sure what I'd have done without you."

Susan nodded and took another deep breath before standing up herself. "I'll be in in just a minute."

She waited until Nicole was gone, then walked down the steps into the garden – admiring the space, but contemplating just how much work the place would need doing. When she turned back to the house, though, something caught her eye, upstairs in the right-hand window. The young girl was there again, the one she'd seen all those years before; Susan recognised her mop of curly hair immediately. She stared at the girl for a moment, and then waved up at her. The girl didn't wave back – but perhaps, Susan thought, it wasn't reasonable to expect she would.

She closed her eyes against the sunlight. When she opened them again, the girl was gone.

Later that night, when Susan had gone home and Louise was asleep across the hall, Nicole walked into her bedroom and saw Jessica, standing by the window with her back to the door.

She's not real, Nicole reminded herself. *This isn't real.*

"I know you're dead," she said aloud. "I know this isn't real."

Nicole turned around, preparing to walk away, but Jessica turned too, reaching out for Nicole's arm and holding her where she stood. Nicole looked down, her mouth open. "I know you died," she whispered. "I know this is in my head."

Jessica smiled, nothing but tenderness in her face. "Nicole? I'm not in your head."

"What is this?" Nicole said. "I don't understand. Louise is here. She told me what happened – reminded me. I know I was making you up, in my head. I know you're not really here anymore."

"I'm here. I've been here since the accident."

Nicole hesitated, not letting herself believe.

"If that's true," she said, haltingly, "if you've really been here all this time… why wouldn't you say something? Why wouldn't you…?"

"I couldn't. How could I talk to you? You weren't ready, Nick. That's why I only came to visit you at night. That's the only time people can see us – me and the other girls. During the day…well, I suppose you know now: that wasn't me. That *was* in your head. I had to let you get through that – mourning, grieving. And I knew that woman Susan would help. When *she* realised I was dead, she didn't run from you or the house; she came over every day to garden with you and clean and drink tea." Jessica rested a hand on

Nicole's waist; stroked a thumb over the exposed skin of Nicole's midriff, the way she always had. "I didn't realise you drank so much tea."

Nicole physically shook at the feel of her touch. "Am I losing my mind?" she said.

Jessica reached up and, with the same thumb, began stroking Nicole's temple instead. "No, sweetheart, you're not losing your mind. It's me, I'm here. Just.... not for long."

"I don't want you to go again," Nicole said – sounding every bit as small and lost as she felt. "It was so hard, losing you. The hardest thing I've ever had to do. I can't do it again."

"You'll have me – you'll always have me. And it wasn't your fault – I hope you know that now. The accident, I mean. It wasn't your fault."

Nicole slumped to her knees. "I'm so sorry," she said, and she was sobbing now, the guilt and the pain and the energy she'd spent conjuring Jessica back to life leeching from her, swirling around her body like a vortex. "I couldn't do it, couldn't save you. I couldn't help."

Jessica kneeled down beside her. "You have to let it go. You have to let *me* go."

"I can't."

"You can. You will. No one stays here forever, Nick. We're all just... coming and going."

"I don't *want* to do this without you, though. Where you are – that's where I need to be."

"I'm not gone, not as long as you remember me. I'll just be...reading in the other room, that's all."

Nicole couldn't stop crying; couldn't let go. Not of Jess; not of the life they'd planned together.

"You have to forgive yourself," Jess repeated. "You have to. You've got the rest of your life to live, and you can't do that if you're mourning mine."

Nicole forced herself to nod.

"I need you to do something else for me, too," Jess added. "Or... for us."

Nicole looked up at her, confused. "Us?"

"Yes. Belle, Olivia, Sinead and Ruth – I believe you've met some of them? They need help. They're... stuck. Here, in the house."

Nicole was speechless, but as it turned out, didn't really need to say anything. Jess, after all, always could read her mind.

"Don't look at me like that," Jess said. "Just because you don't believe in something doesn't mean it doesn't exist."

Nicole wiped her eyes and took a deep breath. "Yes," she said. "I've heard that before, actually. Okay, then. Tell me. What do you need me to do?"

CHAPTER 22

2018

"I've found her!" Susan billowed into the kitchen, at exactly the moment Nicole and Louise had chosen to sit down to lunch.

"Does she have a key?" Louise whispered.

Nicole shrugged, by way of an apology.

"Sister Tabitha Ryan," Susan said. "I've found her."

Truth be told, Nicole hadn't given the nun they'd talked about a second thought; considering what else had been going on, an octogenarian former cloistress she'd never met felt a lower priority than it had.

And Nicole had her own instructions, now. Jess had given them to her the night before, and Nicole knew now where she needed to look, what she needed to do. There would be some work involved, though – and Susan's Michael, when he came back from visiting his friend in Dublin, would be coming 'round to help her with it. To help lay the ghosts of Montpellier Street to rest.

Susan had flicked on the kettle and settled herself at the table beside Louise before either sister could extend the invitation. "I put the word out about her in Mass," she said, "to see if I could track her down. And sure enough, Agnes from over the road knew a woman who knows a woman who works in Hawthorn House." She clapped her hands together triumphantly, then stared Louise and Nicole, in anticipation of their reaction. The younger women exchanged quizzical glances.

"The what?" Nicole asked

"Hawthorn House, love," Susan said. "The hospice out in Roundwood. She's in there, in the hospice – Tabitha Ryan. Sorry, I should've mentioned that bit – I got excited." She stood up again, the rapid motion of her body unsettling Nicole, and positioned herself at the counter to make the tea. "So we're going to visit her today," she added.

Nicole hadn't told Susan – or Louise, for that matter – what Jess had said. Susan might believe in ghosts, Louise absolutely didn't – and even if she were to start, it was too soon, too implausible, coming on the heels of their discovery of Nicole's unravelling. The last thing Nicole wanted was for either of them to worry; they were already walking on eggshells around her, treating her as if she might break again at any moment.

She wouldn't need them for the plan, fortunately. Not with Michael there. She'd let him in, get him to look at the wiring in the basement... and then, *then* she'd be able do what Jess had asked of her.

"You want us to go and see a nun in a hospice, today?" Louise sounded incredulous, which, Nicole reasoned, was fair, given the total lack of context in Susan's announcement.

"Tabitha was a nun back in the fifties," she explained, before Susan could step in and complicate things further. "We think she lived – or at least worked – in this house. In 1955, she left the nuns, but Susan's convinced she can tell us what went on with the house, and why the girls are still...you know...around."

"I see," Louise said, still sceptical.

"You don't have to come," Nicole added – reassuringly, or so she hoped.

S usan was as eager as ever on the way to Roundwood. If anything, she was more enthusiastic even than usual.

"What should we ask her?" she was saying as she drove, tapping at the steering wheel like a woman who'd had one too many cups of tea. "Should we go good cop, bad cop?"

"Jesus, Susan," Nicole told her. "The woman's eighty-odd. If anything, we should keep our voices down and hope she doesn't die while we're there."

"Ah, the softly, softly approach. I like it."

Nicole let out a little sigh of frustration. "Look, we just need to ask her a few questions and try not upset her. I want to know if she knew anything about the girls staying in the house. And if that goes well, maybe we'll ask her why she left the nunnery."

Susan nodded, her eyes fixed now on the road ahead. "Okay. Got it."

Nicole studied her. "Maybe," she said, "you should let me do the talking..."

Roundwood was a seaside village on the west coast of the city: quaint and beautiful, its main street decorated with row upon row of the kind of brightly-decorated shops that drew in the American tourists who flocked to Galway in summertime, anxious to explore their Irish heritage. Today, though, it was quiet; there were only locals around, most of them farmers moving their cattle from one field to another.

Susan's hands still pounding a staccato rhythm on the wheel, they drove through the village, emerging by the windswept Atlantic on the other side. Hawthorn House was perched on a hill overlooking the ocean – a sprawling, charmless, weather-beaten single-storey surrounded by high fences, the only entrance a wide gate at the front of the property.

They left the car on the pavement outside and headed in, past the gate and the unexpectedly open main door.

At the front desk, they were greeted by a lady of formidable countenance whose light blue name badge identified her as Nurse Maguire. "Yes?" she asked them, not a trace of warmth or patience in her greeting.

"Good afternoon," Nicole said. "We're here to see Tabitha Ryan." She smiled; a doomed attempt at thawing the already-frosty atmosphere.

"And who are you to Ms Ryan, exactly?" came the reply. "Are you a relation? I don't see your name in the visitor book, and we take the security of our guests very seriously."

Susan stepped forward. "I'm Deborah Marshal," she said, in a drawling but regionally-indeterminate American accent, "and I've travelled all the way from Boston to see Cousin Tabby. It would just be swell if you could show us to her room."

Nicole glared at Susan, who remained unflustered, maintaining eye contact with Nurse Maguire.

"I see. " The nurse paused. "Well..."

"Deborah," Susan prompted, the accent growing more questionable by the second.

"...Deborah, you understand I'm going to have to check with Ms Ryan, to make sure she's happy to receive you?"

Susan was flummoxed, momentarily. Then Deborah came roaring back to life and took the reins. "Oh, sweetness – she isn't going to remember me. Good God, it's been decades, and Cousin Tabby is up in her eighties now. Last time I saw her was in London, maybe thirty years ago. And I hear her memory now isn't what it used to be."

It was a hell of a risk. They knew nothing about the old nun's recall, her cognitive abilities. For all they knew, she could've been in the back dancing the Charleston and reciting Ulysses from memory.

Nurse Maguire considered this. "Yes," she said. "She *has* been struggling to remember things lately, but I do believe she was in London around that time. Listen: she doesn't have very many visitors, apart from her two nun friends, so I'll let you down to see her. But if she becomes even slightly distressed, I'm going to need you ladies to leave. Are we clear?"

"Crystal, my dear," Susan responded, in an accent that was becoming more South Carolina and less Boston by the second.

"Thank you," Nicole added but the nurse had already disappeared from the desk and was making her way out into the lobby.

"This way, ladies," she told them, strutting purposefully ahead of them, her bright white shoes squeaking like unoiled brakes on the laminate flooring.

They followed her, down a long white corridor, past several rooms with ominously closed doors . Nicole kept her eyes ahead. She wasn't a fan of hospitals, not since the accident; and though this one was a care facility, the noises and the smells, the entropy in the air were much the same.

At the front desk, a telephone began to ring.

Nurse Maguire ground to a halt at the sound and swivelled round to face them with the speed of an ice-dancer.

"I should get that," she said. "We're expecting a new patient today. Can you ladies find your own way from here? It's straight down to the end, then the first door on your right – number seventeen."

"But of course, my dear," Susan assured her. "You get on, and we'll find our way to Cousin Tabby." The accent was close to crossing the Atlantic by now; Nicole wished she'd keep her sentences shorter.

Nurse Maguire stared at her for a moment and then glanced back at Nicole.

"Right," she said. "Just remember – the slightest bit of distress, and you need to leave. Okay?"

And with that, she left.

"What the hell was all that?" Nicole asked Susan, when she was sure the nurse was out of earshot.

"It got us in, didn't it? I thought I did rather well. Didn't you like my American accent?"

Nicole rolled her eyes. "Yes, all *three* of them were very impressive. Perhaps next time, you could just... pick the one and stick to it? Anyway. Do you want to find this nun? Then we can get out of here, once we've spoken to her. This place is giving me the creeps."

Susan nodded.

They followed Nurse Maguire's instructions, all the way to Tabitha's door.

"Here we go," Nicole said. "And would you mind going back to your real accent? We don't want her any more confused than she is already."

"Fine," Susan said. But Nicole got the impression she was sulking as they knocked on the door.

No answer came from inside.

"Do you think she's asleep?" Nicole asked.

Susan sighed. "Well, that would be disappointing, wouldn't it, after we've driven all this way?" With that, she opened the door a sliver, and coughed, loudly.

"Jesus, Susan!" Nicole said.

"Hello, who's there?" asked a frail voice from behind the door.

"See?" Susan hissed. "She's up."

She pushed the door open wider and strode inside, more confidently than entirely necessary. "Good afternoon, Ms Ryan!" she boomed into the room. "I'm Susan, and this is Nicole. How are you feeling today?"

The old lady sat low in the bed, pillows stacked behind her in a sunken heap. The atmosphere in the room was heavy; stale. Ryan herself looked frail, her thinning grey hair stuck to her scalp and her eyes set back in their sockets. The sight of her, and the room, seemed to kick-start Susan into action; before Nicole knew what was happening, before she could even step inside the room, the older woman had the window open and was plumping pillows behind the old nun's back.

"I'm okay, I suppose." Ryan eyed them suspiciously. Do I know you?"

Nicole answered before Susan had the chance to. "No, you don't know us. We're here to ask you some questions, Ms Ryan."

"Yes," Susan added. "Questions about something we're looking into, from a long time back. You might not remember – it's to do with a house you once lived in, on Montpellier Street."

Tabatha pushed herself upright in the bed.

"Ah, I see," she said, with sudden dignity. "Well... I've been waiting for you."

"*Waiting* for us?" Nicole shot a glance at Susan, who looked equally bewildered.

"Yes, and for quite some time, too. I assume you're here to arrest me?"

CHAPTER 23

2018

"**A**rrest you?" Nicole asked the nun, surprised. "Arrest you for what?"

The former Sister Tabitha wavered. "Are you... not the Gardai?"

"No, no we're not," said Susan. "I live on Montpellier Street, and Nicole here is my neighbour. She bought number 17, and we heard you lived there once, or worked there? There've been some... strange goings on in the house, and we thought you might be able to shed some light on them."

"I see." Ryan turned her attention to Nicole. "So, you live there...in that house?"

"Yes," Nicole told her. "And as Susan said, there've been some unusual... sightings."

"What kind of sightings?" The old woman seemed unconcerned by this – curious, but not alarmed.

"You might not believe this," Nicole said – quickly, before she lost her nerve, "but there are ghosts in the house."

Susan nodded her agreement. "Three of them, we think. All girls, Ms Ryan."

"Call me Tabby," the old nun said. "And yes, that sounds about right. Though I'm surprised there's only three."

Nicole's pulsed quickened.

"You knew them?" she asked, faltering. "The girls? You know what happened to them?"

"I'm rather afraid I do, yes." Ryan – *Tabby* – looked down at her bony, frail hands, her arthritic fingers worrying at the crochet blanket draped over her lap.

A hundred questions assailed Nicole. She settled, finally, on the one bothering her the most. "Why did you think we came here to arrest you?"

Tabby looked up from her hands. "It's a bit of a long story, my dear. Why don't you both take a seat and I'll tell you all about it?" She gestured to the cheap, antimacassar-covered armchairs on either side of the bed, and Nicole lowered herself into one of them, warily.

"Now," Tabby said, "I suppose, before I get to why I thought you were here, I should start back a bit, to 1955. I was twenty-one then, and green as a blade of grass. Brand-new to the nunnery... and with no idea how much evil I'd encounter, in my short time as a Bride of Christ."

"Come along, Sister Tabitha," the Mother Superior chided. "Why must you always insist on being late for everything?"

"I'm sorry, Sister Fitzgerald," Tabby said. "My stocking ripped, and I couldn't find..."

"My child, I couldn't care less about your excuses, and I doubt the good Lord has any interest in your undergarments. Prayers have already begun."

Tabby hated Sister Fitz. Well... perhaps didn't hate her – she shouldn't *hate* anyone, should she? But she was terrified of her, that was for certain. The older nun was mean and hateful, and for no other reason than that she could be; there was no-one around to challenge her or hold her to account. Tabby hated the way she spoke to the girls; as if she *wanted* them to feel bad. What was the point in that? Even if some of them had made mistakes, God was there to forgive, wasn't he? Not to judge. But Sister Mary Agnes Fitzgerald acted as if she'd been reading all her life from a different Bible.

She was physically abusive to the girls, too; another manifestation of her vicious streak, one Tabby found even less acceptable than the casual cruelty.

Tabby had been delighted, therefore, when she was offered a new post, away from Sister Fitzgerald and the constant threat of ridicule she represented: in a new house, just up the way.

When, the morning after the incident with the torn stockings, Tabby arrived there, she was brimming with excitement. She hadn't been told much about the post – but she knew there'd be a doctor there, and she'd be helping him manage and treat the small number of girls already living on Montpellier Street. She knew one of them quite well already, in fact, from her time at the main house. The girl's name was Belle, and she suffered badly from fits. Having seen it happen first-hand, Tabby was hopeful the doctor could help her.

The first thing she noticed, as the car pulled up in front of the building, was how clean and bright the new house was, all freshly painted and decorated. There were steps leading up to a beautiful green door; just the look of them made Tabby giddy at the prospect of her new beginning.

Inside, she was introduced to Dr Baker, a very well-spoken English gentleman, and she found herself utterly charmed. He was to live in the house with her, though Father Jameson would come and go. There would be only three of them there full-time, at first – Tabby, Belle and Baker. She and Belle were confused, therefore, on opening the wardrobe in Tabby's bedroom upstairs, and discovering a cache of women's clothing, seemingly abandoned.

Tabby asked the doctor where they'd come from, who they'd belonged to. But he'd been less than forthcoming; had told them instead that they could throw them out or give them to the girls in the main house, but that they were never to be worn in Montpellier Street. And that he had no wish to ever set eyes on them again.

"Things started to go wrong almost immediately." Tabby was still fidgeting with the blanket on her lap, her voice weak.

"What do you mean?" Susan asked.

"Well, the course of treatment the doctor recommended for Belle was... bizarre. Or so I thought at the time. *Experimental* might be a better way to put it now."

"Oh, God – did he take out her eyes?" Nicole asked in a whisper – flashing back to the girl in her bed, the bloody voids where her eyes should have been.

Tabby looked up at her in surprise. "No – but how did you...?"

"I've met her, I think – kind of."

Tabby stared at her, speechless, until Susan touched her hand, encouraging her to speak again.

"I see," she said. "Well, poor Belle did that to herself – but only after weeks of sleep deprivation. It was practically torture, now I look back on it." The old woman closed her own eyes for a moment. "Who else have you... met? Can you describe the other girls you've seen?"

"Olivia was first." Nicole stopped; thought. "She told me her name. I saw her in the upstairs bathroom."

The old woman's face grew even more ashen than before, and what had been a faint tremor in her hands grew stronger, until it seemed her whole body was shaking.

Susan stood up immediately, and was over to Tabby in a flash, stroking the old nun's arm. "Are you alright, love? Here, take a nice deep breath into you. You're alright, you're safe."

Nicole could only admire Susan's instinct to protect, to soothe.

"I'm okay," Tabby said, her voice as tremulous as the rest of her. "I only found out after I'd left that she died there. Dr Baker... he told me she'd had been transferred." She sounded, Nicole thought, every one of her eighty-three years now, and frightened. "He really was a *monster*," she added, more firmly.

"I'm sorry," Nicole offered. Then: "So, there was Olivia – she slit her throat in the upstairs bathroom."

"Nicole," Susan said, "perhaps we can just stick to the names we know for now, and maybe a physical description? I don't think Tabby needs to know all the details." Susan was glaring at her, Nicole saw; chastising her.

"Right, sorry. Of course. Okay, so there was Olivia in the upstairs bathroom. Then Belle in the upstairs bedroom... and Susan saw another girl in the back bedroom. But you only saw her from the back garden through the window, isn't that right, Susan?"

"Yes," Susan confirmed, her hand still resting on Tabby's arm. "She had a lot of curly hair, much like my own, and she was looking out the window onto the back steps."

"That was Sinead," Tabby said quietly. "She let herself fall out of that window and to her death on those very steps. That was the beginning of the end for me, the day she died. It was one of the worst days of my life, and it changed the course of it – changed me – forever."

Tabby knew almost immediately something was wrong when she pulled into the drive. She could see the little window to the basement had been smashed, the sun glistening on the shards left scattered across the gravel. But before she was able to walk around the side of the house to inspect the damage, she heard the doctor shouting out to her from the porch.

"Where have you been, woman? Get in here at once."

"Yes, sorry, Doctor Baker," she told him, instinctively deferential. "I got delayed at the markets…"

She took a proper look, and her apologies fell away. He was soaked in blood, his white shirt drenched in it; his eyes were manic, the pupils so dilated they looked black as a shark's. His dark hair, normally slicked back and neat, had broken off from his scalp in greasy strands. He looked not just dishevelled, but deranged.

"What happened?" she asked him, fearing the worst. "Are you okay? Should I call for an ambulance?"

"You should come inside – now," he snarled back at her. Then turned on his heel and headed back into the house.

At the bottom of the steps, she hesitated, every bone in her body telling her to get back in the car and drive away. She didn't, though.

Naïve as she was back then, she thought: *he needs help. Somebody in there needs help.*

And so she followed him, up the steps and into the house.

She found Father Jameson inside, huddled in the hallway while Dr Baker paced the floor, more agitated – if such a thing were possible – even than he'd been on the steps.

"Did you see them?" Baker demanded. "On your way from town, did you see them along the road?"

Tabby was too scared to reply. Father Jameson, she noticed, was also silent: leaning up against the staircase with his hand on his stomach, looking to Tabby as if he might be sick at any moment.

"*Did you see them?*" Baker repeated.

"See *who*, Doctor?" Tabby said, finding her voice. "What are you talking about? And why are you covered in blood? Is someone hurt?"

"Grace and Ellen!" Baker told her. "They've run off. We need to find them, get them back."

But why would the girls do that? she thought – knowing better than to pose the question aloud. Neither Grace nor Ellen had ever struck her as the volatile type. "Doctor?" she asked instead. "Whose blood is that, on your shirt? Where did it come from?"

Doctor Baker looked down at his clothes and hands, as if observing them for the very first time. "Oh, don't worry about her," he said softly. "She's already dead".

Every hair rose on the back of Tabby's neck. Her palms began to sweat, Baker's words – their meaning – ricocheting around her head. *She's dead. She's already dead.*

She pushed past him, ignoring his muttered protests; sidestepping the priest, who looked himself as white as a ghost now, and darting towards the kitchen.

There were footprints on the tiles there, ragged and bloody, tracking towards her from the other directions. She followed them, out through the back door, and saw the sheets: bright white but similarly spattered with blood.

And the girl's body on the pathway: broken and crumpled and sodden with gore.

A red smear unfurled from her like a ribbon – travelling midway down the steps, as if someone had dragged her body down from them and pulled her onto the pathway before giving up and leaving her there, discarded.

Tabby felt her gorge rising; tasted acid in her throat. She swallowed it down. There was no time to vomit: whatever she did next, she'd need to do it quickly.

She approached the body – tentatively, careful not to get too close to the ruined face, the wild hair matted with drying blood. There was something on the ground by the girl's body, she noticed: the St. Brigid's cross Sinead wore around her neck. It must have come loose when whoever moved her had dragged her down the steps. Tabby bent down and picked it up; cleaned it off with her sleeve, and placed it carefully in her pocket.

In a daze, she returned to the kitchen. The priest was there now, waiting for her – though Baker was nowhere to be seen.

"Father Jameson, what in God's name's been happening here? Have you been outside? Sinead – she's dead."

"He killed them," the priest muttered, apparently in shock himself.

"Killed *them*? What does that mean, that there were others? Speak to me, Father. Who else did he kill?"

The priest swayed against the counter and put his hand back to steady himself.

"Father?" she pressed, cognisant of his discomfort but refusing to entertain it. "*Who else?*"

He cast his eyes up to the ceiling, as if he were speaking not to Tabby but to God Himself. "Not her," he said. "Not Sinead. She jumped." His voice cracked. "Ruth, Sister – Ruth and the baby, her wee one. He killed them. Murdered them both."

At this, the priest broke down completely, sinking to his knees on the cold, hard floor.

"Ruth is *dead*?" Tabby said.

The priest nodded; pointing beyond the kitchen, to the basement door.

"Down there," he said, though she could barely hear him through his weeping. "In the basement. Look yourself, and you'll find her."

CHAPTER 24

2018

"But from the way you were talking, I assumed you'd, you know... *done* something. Something bad enough for people to want to arrest you." Nicole said.

"Not then," Tabby said. "I didn't do anything *then*. But later... well, I suppose we'll come to that."

"Where did you go?" Susan was still stroking Tabby's arm, as gently as before, but there was more than a glimmer of curiosity in her eyes now, too.

Tabby leaned back into her pillows. "Well, I didn't leave right away, if that's what you're asking. I went outside and around the house, to where the glass was broken. I wanted to look into the basement – I needed to know; you understand. To see for myself. And I *did* see, when I looked in: saw Doctor Baker, dragging the body along the ground. Ruth's body, I should say. And she *was* dead, of course. There was a great wooden stake thing jutting out of her throat."

"Good God," Susan said. "And the girl was pregnant, you say?"

The nun nodded, still visibly wracked with anguish – as if Ruth had died yesterday, and not 60 years ago or more. "Yes. Due any day then, from what I recall."

"About that, Tabby," Nicole said – cautiously, awkwardly, but mindful of the need to know, after Nurse Maguire's observation. "How *is* your memory these days?"

Susan tutted. Tabby, however, seemed unfazed by the question.

"I have good days and bad days, my dear. Sometimes I forget what I had for breakfast, or what days my programmes are on – but I assure you, seeing a heavily pregnant woman with her throat ripped open is something that stays with you."

Nicole swallowed, embarrassed. "Of course. I'm sorry, Tabby. I didn't mean to interrupt."

The nun smiled at her, forgivingly. "That's quite all right, dear. As I was saying, though: I *did* see her, down there. And of course, *then* I ran. I had no idea where I was going, not at first, but I knew I had to get away. I was afraid to go straight to the Gardai. Doctors and priests... they could do no wrong, back then – and there I was, still a child myself, getting ready to spin them some story about a doctor murdering a pregnant girl and a priest standing by while he did it? Sure, I would have been locked up; that was the power they had. The law didn't exist for men like that, not in those days."

"Sounds like you were so lucky to get away," Nicole said. "Did you hear about Father Jameson, though?" she added. "About what happened to him?"

"That he hanged himself? I did, I did hear that. Sure, the man was riddled with guilt – who could ever be right after that? It was his gambling debts that let that snake Baker in the door – and him not even a real doctor, as I heard it. He was already disgraced over the water in England."

"Whatever became of him?" Susan asked. "He'd be long dead by now, but what did he do after all that in '55?"

The old nun shifted slightly in her bed.

"Well... first, I decided to make some calls. I called the Guards – anonymously, of course. Not that I thought they'd listen. But I called them, and said they needed to get to Montpellier Street straight away, that there'd been a murder. I heard years later someone *did* call 'round, but Baker saw whoever it was off on the porch. He must have cleaned himself up by then, because I believe it was laughed off, right there at the door – as a hoax, or some other such nonsense. No Guard ever entered the premises, as far as I know.

I made calls to the monastery, too: to the archbishop's offices, telling them what had happened, though I didn't give a name then, either. It was too risky. Nothing ever came of it. And if anyone *did* find anything out, it was brushed under the carpet. The Catholic Church has a way of protecting itself, doesn't it? Even to the detriment of what's good. All it cares about is its own survival – that's always been the most important thing. Anything that threatens that, they remove. Or ship off to another country."

Tabby let out a loud, crackling cough, and Susan reached for the water jug.

"Do you need to take a break?" she said. "We can come back another day if you need to rest."

Tabby smiled, the wrinkles in her face deepening. "At my age, dear, it's foolish to assume there'll *be* another day. Besides, I'm getting to the important part."

Susan sat back down. Tabby took several long sips of water and readjusted her position in the bed.

"It was clear to me after a while that nothing was going to happen; nobody was going to intercede. I never went back to number 17, or to the main house, but I stayed in town for a couple of weeks – long enough to hear about Father Jameson crawling out onto the windowsill of the upstairs bedroom with six feet of rope." She paused for a moment; blessed herself, and carried on. "He wasn't a bad man, Father Jameson. Just a broken one, and that was how he died, broken. Now, Baker... I tried to keep track of him. He went to Dublin after he left here, you know? I went there myself, but truth be told, I was going to Dublin anyway. I had a cousin there, and she'd arranged to get me a job as a housemaid. I couldn't carry on as a nun, not after what I'd seen."

"Well, I don't think anyone could blame you there, Tabby," Susan told her. "It was a horrific thing to go through, just horrific. You're a brave woman, make no mistake about it."

"You're very kind," Tabby said, with a little squeeze of Susan's hand. Then: "I stayed in Dublin for five years after that: worked a couple of housemaid jobs for some rich Dublin folk and tried to put it all behind me, what I'd seen. Then in January of '61 I made the move to London – and a big move it was, too. I'd met a lovely family back in Dublin, the Murphys: she was English, and he was Irish. Jacob Murphy, that was his name; he had a fine set of teeth on him." Tabby glanced at Nicole, appearing faintly embarrassed by the admission. "It's funny the things that stay with you. But they needed a nanny, and I'd always loved children, so I jumped at the chance, and off I went to London. Leaving all my troubles behind, or so I thought. I'm ashamed to say it, but apart from a few nightmares every now and again, I didn't really think much about Galway. I tried not to, anyway. But the past doesn't work like that, does it? So it was, one day in late January, that my own past ran into me – quite literally."

"**A**re you sure you don't mind? I don't have to go."

"Will you please just run on, Tabby," Jacob said, his Donegal accent thick as ever. "You deserve a night out and, sure, aren't they our wains anyway?"

They'd been in London almost three weeks, and it was the first night she'd had off since they'd arrived – but still, she felt guilty for abandoning her employers.

"Okay," she conceded. "But I won't be too late, and I have a key. I'll be fine to get up with them in the morning."

She grabbed her wool coat and scarf on the way out, wrapping herself up against the elements. There was a light rain, but she didn't have too far to walk to the Tube station. She'd get the Tube to Chelsea from Hammersmith; that was the plan. Then go the rest of the way to the pub on foot. It wouldn't take her long.

It was on the platform at Chelsea she first saw him, or thought she did: a vision from the past, from Galway and Montpellier Street. But the glimpse was so brief, and the look of him so generic, she felt sure she must have been mistaken. Slicked-back hair, a cheap suit and confident walk: men like that were ten-a-penny in London.

It wasn't Baker, she thought – shaking off the temporary shock that had run through her at the sight of the man and climbing the stairs to the damp street above. It couldn't be Baker.

The pub where she'd be meeting Wendy and Charlotte, the new friends she made at the school gates – both of them nannies, like her – was only two streets over from the station; she'd never been there before, but the girls had given her clear directions, so it was easy enough to find. She was fiddling with her wet umbrella outside the place, distracted, when she and the same gentleman collided; he'd been right in front of her, she realised later, doing the same thing with an umbrella of his own. The collision was wholly unceremonious.

"Oh, my goodness!" Tabby exclaimed. "I'm so sorry."

"You should be more careful, my dear," the man told her, more condescending than angry. "And watch where you're going next time."

Tabby didn't look up at him right away, distracted as she was by disentangling her umbrella and fixing her hair.

When eventually she did, her breath caught in her throat.

"Did you hear me?" the man said. "I said, you should be more careful."

It can't be, Tabby thought. *It can't be him: not now, not here.*

It was, though; there could be no doubt about it. It was Baker: there, in the flesh, in London, just as she was.

"Girl? Are you mute?" He was growing irritated now, already weary of their interaction; little slivers of the anger she'd known so well beginning to seep out from the edges of his pristine façade.

"Yes! I mean no. I mean..." Tabby steadied herself. "Yes, I can hear you. And no I'm not a mute."

She dipped her head low, the better to shield herself from him. It was clear he hadn't recognised her, and she was keen to keep it that way.

"I'm fine," she said. "Sorry for bumping into you. I must get on, I'm late to meet my friends." She motioned to the door of the pub.

"Ah, yes – I'm going here too." Baker reached across her and pulled open the large wooden door by its brass handle. "After you," he said, standing back and ushering Tabby through with his free hand.

She walked towards him, her head down. She was only inches from him now, and the proximity set her whole body on edge. She felt the hair rise on her neck, and flashed back suddenly to the last day she'd spent in his company: his white shirt blood-soaked and murder in his eyes. It was unbearable. She wanted to turn, to run, to scream.

Instead, she stepped inside.

"Thank you," she said, just loud enough for him to hear – and escaped into the crowd.

"So he was there? In London?" Susan was practically falling off her chair in her excitement.

"He was," Tabby told her. "And isn't it just sod's law that I'd run right into him?"

"You were lucky he didn't recognise you," Nicole said.

"Well, I looked very different in 1961 than I had in the '50s. That's the thing about being a nun – people don't look past the clothes. They see the habit, never the woman. I did see him again, though, as it happened. Several times."

Days passed, but Tabby still couldn't rid herself of the thought of him. She saw him in every stranger's face: at the park, in the butcher's shop, by the school gates. He invoked in her, the same fear and anxiety he had in Montpellier Street, the same helplessness, and it infuriated her. She'd spent so long, invested so much effort into moving on – and now here she was again, haunted. Haunted by the girls, by Ruth and her unborn baby. It ate away at her, the idea of him free, unburdened; strolling through Chelsea, drinking in pubs, while those girls – those *children* – lay dead at his hand. She couldn't let their story end that way.

He was an evil man; and evil men, she was sure, didn't just change their ways. What was he doing now? Where was he staying, how was he paying his way, with whom was he mixing? How was he living with himself? She had to know.

But how?

A few weeks later and another chance for her to visit the pub arose. There was no guarantee Baker would be there, of course – but it was a place to start.

She sat alone at the bar that night for almost an hour, rebuffing the advances of those young men who took her aloneness as a sign to approach her, and avoiding the eye of the landlord, who viewed her throughout with undisguised suspicion. She was cursing herself for not arranging to meet friends when the door of the pub opened, letting in a blast of cool February air that scuttled like mice around her ankles. And there Baker was, as if he knew she'd been waiting for him.

He strode up to the bar, removed his hat and ordered a brandy with a splash of ginger ale, oblivious to her presence.

She didn't have a plan – only watched as the bartender put the drink down in front of Baker. The Doctor, true to form, picked it up without thanks. After a few minutes, another man came and sat beside him; they nodded to one another, though it wasn't clear to Tabby if they knew each other, or if they were simply being polite. The second gentleman was well-to-do, if his well-shone shoes and silk necktie were any indication. It wasn't that he was dressed differently to the other men in the bar, she thought. Simply that he was dressed...better: his shirt a finer quality of cloth, his shoes made of a softer leather. Tabby's uncle had been a tailor in County Clare, where she'd grown up – and while she had no interest herself in fancy clothes, she could recognise good craftmanship when she saw it.

The second man didn't order a drink. Instead he waved the bartender away, reached into his jacket and took out a white envelope, small but bulky, and placed it on the bar beside his elbow. Baker, as if on cue, picked up the envelope with one hand and slid it inside the outer pocket of his overcoat – all while sipping his brandy with the other, unoccupied hand. If Tabby hadn't been watching their interaction, and watching it intently, she'd never have noticed the transaction. By the time Baker had replaced the empty brandy glass back on the bar, the other man was already sliding off his stool and walking to the door; a moment later Baker, his business and his brandy both concluded, laid a handful of coins on the counter and readied himself to leave.

Tabby slipped her arms into her coat. When Baker got up and made for the exit, she went after him – using a crowd of men apparently on a pub crawl as cover. They fell out into the street in an impromptu conga line, and she fell in behind them; then, in the darkness of the evening, her eyes trained on the outline of Baker's umbrella, she followed him home.

What are you doing? a part of her screamed. *This is madness.*

But she kept on, stalking him as he walked – though from what she hoped was a safe distance. He ambled along the pavements, over cobblestones, weaving in and out of streets, until he stopped at a narrow townhouse: three storeys high, black railings lining the steps leading up to the red door. Number 8, the brass plaque by the doorbell read; Number 8, Mason Gardens.

He took a bundle of keys from his overcoat and, after a brief look around him, put one of the keys in the lock, opened the door and stepped inside.

And now, she thought, *I know where you live.*

Whenever she could, over the next few weeks, she passed by Mason Gardens in search of him. What she really wanted to know, she'd discovered, was how he was making his money. His delusions of grandeur notwithstanding, he was just a disgraced doctor – who would hire him? What lies was he telling to get by? She'd seen women coming in and going from the house – sometimes in the company of men, sometimes not. The building itself was plain, had no real signage, so whatever Baker was doing, he wasn't advertising his services.

She'd follow one of the girls, she decided. If she could just strike up a conversation with one of them, just once, then perhaps Tabby could learn what he was up to.

She had to wait another week after that to find a girl – one leaving the house on her own. She was eighteen or so, in Tabby's estimation – definitely not much older. For someone her age, though, she walked with some difficulty: her pace slow and laboured as she shuffled down the stairs, and her posture crooked when she paused on the bottom step to gather herself. She was obviously struggling, and eventually Tabby decided to intervene; she could ask her questions and help the girl at the same time, after all.

"Are you okay?" she asked the girl, coming up alongside her.

The girl looked startled. "I'm fine, thank you," she replied, eyeing Tabby with suspicion.

"Are you sure? You look like you could do with a hand."

The girl was wearing a long overcoat, but Tabby could see she was holding her stomach.

"Are you in pain?"

"No," the girl said. "I'm fine, really. I just hurt my ankle is all – it's hard to put weight on it." The girl forced a smile. "But thank you for asking."

She began to walk away, with evident difficulty.

"Was that why you went to see Doctor Baker?" Tabby called after her. "Because you'd hurt your ankle?"

The girl stopped still and turned slowly around to face Tabby. "What did you just say?"

"Doctor Baker? The man you saw about your ankle. He's not a real doctor, you know."

Fear and anger – and something like shame – crossed the woman's face.

"Were you following me?" she said.

"Not exactly." Tabby moved closer towards her, and lowered her voice. "I'm more interested in Baker. But I saw you leave there a moment ago, so I suppose... technically, yes, I *am* following you. And you look as if you might need help."

"All I *need*," the girl told her, forcefully, "is for you to leave me alone."

She quickened her pace, and Tabby let her go. She'd only wanted to warn the girl, in any case: to tell her Baker wasn't who he said he was, wasn't a real doctor. Something bothered Tabby, though. And against all reason, she found herself not walking back to her own home, but tailing the girl, through three more streets, all the way to a run down-looking building off the King's Road, where the girl let herself into a small basement flat and, in doing so, disappeared from view.

Tabby didn't sleep well that night, nor the night after. The nebulous *something* that had troubled her when she'd confronted the girl continued to nag at her, to keep her from resting. Perhaps, she thought, it would help if she could see the girl again, ask her for more details about Baker - and what else but a twisted ankle Baker might be treating her for – in a way that didn't antagonise her or cause her to flee.

So it was that, the morning after a third sleepless night – with the Murphy children safely deposited at school – Tabby boarded a bus to the King's Road and, from there, retraced her steps to the girl's dilapidated block of flats.

Her visit wouldn't be well-received, she knew. But she'd never forgive herself for not reaching out to the girl. Not after Montpellier Street. Not after Ruth.

She made no attempt to gain access through the main front entrance of the building. Rather, she took the outside steps to the basement flat and rang the doorbell.

There was no answer.

After a second ring yielded the same result, she considered leaving – coming back another day and trying again then. But then she caught sight of the basement window sitting just to the left of the door, its dirty glass protected by a row of rusty metal bars.

Tabby craned her neck and peered inside.

No, she thought, while inside of her something screamed. *It can't be. Not again.*

The flat was small, dingy – barely more than a bedsit. Through the window, in spite of the bars, she could see straight into the kitchenette – where, on the linoleum floor, the girl lay dead, blood pooled and smeared around her body.

She'd flailed in it, Tabby saw: thrashed around in her blood, her own fluids, like a perverse snow angel. It was everywhere, the blood: not just on the floor, but on the doors of the kitchen cabinets, on the wall above her contorted corpse. Tabby could imagine the girl's final frantic moments all too well: the panic, the fear, the futile efforts she'd made to stop the bleeding between her legs, stemming the flow with towels, blankets... anything she could find. The realisation that she couldn't, wouldn't; that she was going to bleed out, die alone in her bedsit, on a floor she'd meant to mop but never got around to.

The truth was, Tabby thought, she'd been dying from the moment she left Baker's house. Dying when she hobbled down the steps; dying when Tabby had tried in vain to talk to her. Wheels had been set in motion that day, and had culminated in this, here, now: another young woman dead at Baker's indifferent, incompetent hand.

She pulled back from the window and vomited into the hedge.

CHAPTER 25

2018

"Back street abortions?" Susan asked, with a shake of her head.

"I'm afraid so, yes." Tabby was looking tired now, Nicole thought – the reminiscing starting to take its toll.

"Did you report it, what he was doing?" she said. "Did you go to the police?"

"I thought about it, of course. But no, I decided not to. It wasn't just the people who carried out the abortion that were prosecuted, you understand – it was the women, too. I couldn't do that to them. Though... I couldn't let him carry on, either. He was dangerous. He had to be stopped."

"What did you do?" Nicole was beginning to suspect she knew the answer already.

"Well..." The old woman hesitated. "I stopped him, dear."

The nightmares came back more forcefully than ever, after she discovered the body: what she'd witnessed in Galway mingling with images of the girl whose name she didn't know and would likely never know. She knew she had to act – that she couldn't let him go on endangering women, desperate women with nowhere else to turn. But what could she do? Realistically, the only way to get him to stop was to confront him. To blackmail him, if she had to. She knew what he'd done in Ireland: she'd threaten to expose it all, expose *him* if he didn't stop.

It took her another full week to summon up the courage to return to Mason Gardens. She had no real idea what she might say, but she knew his temper; knew it would be folly to find herself alone with him. The conversation, she thought, would need to happen on the doorstep.

"Yes?" Baker said, irritably – swinging upon the door at her knock. "What do you want?" He had one arm in his coat, clearly about to go out.

"I…" she told him, haltingly. "I need to book an appointment."

This hadn't been part of her plan. But she needed his full attention, and the lie had spilled out.

Baker stilled, seeming to examine her properly for the first time. His brow furrowed, and he tilted his head to the side, scanning her features, her body. After what felt like an age, something like realisation dawned.

He recognises you.

"You should come in," he said.

"I'd rather not. I don't intend to keep you very long."

"Well, *I* don't intend to discuss my affairs on the doorstep, so you can come in, or you can go away."

He held open the door, tapping out an impatient rhythm with his foot.

"Fine," she said, her prior resolve thrown suddenly, unexpectedly to the wind. "I'll come in, but I can't stay long."

It was a terrible idea, she was certain of that. But despite her better judgement, she brushed past him and inside. Into the heart of his lair.

"Go through to the kitchen," he told her, the door clicking shut behind him.

The hallway was dark, damp, narrow. Slowly, she walked along it to the kitchen. It was small and dingy, poorly-maintained and badly-lit – with, she noticed, no back door, but a stack of dirty dishes in the sink. On the countertop she saw letters, a pile of them, crowned by a gleaming silver letter opener: its brightness a stark contrast to the filth around it.

With both of them in it, the kitchen felt unbearably cramped. An awkward tension hung in the air between them.

"So – it's you," Baker said. "I didn't recognise you at first, but when you spoke, I knew."

Tabby shuddered. She'd intended to reveal herself to him eventually, of course, so what difference did it make, that he recognised her? She knew that, logically, she ought not to care. But her physical reactions, the shaking and the clamminess of her hands... they told her otherwise.

"You know, then?" she said. "Who I am?"

"Of course. You're that girl, the one who crashed into me outside of the pub a few weeks ago. Now, tell me: how far along are you?"

He doesn't *know*, she thought.

"I'm not pregnant." She spoke slowly, afraid to give him any hint of her unease. "Look again, Doctor. Are you sure you don't recognise me from anywhere else?"

He continued to stare at her, his beady eyes sweeping her face for clues.

"Sister Tabitha," he said eventually.

"It's just Tabby now, but yes. I assume *Mr* Baker will suffice?" He grimaced at the slight, but she ignored it, pressed on. "I think we have some catching up to do, don't you?"

"**G**od, you were so brave," Nicole said, with something like awe. The old lady smiled to herself. "It's the confidence of youth, dear. I was so shy when I joined the nuns, when he knew me. But I'd changed by the sixties. Those years in Dublin, the move to London... they made a big difference to me. I was meeting new people, reading a lot – finding my feet. I'd started questioning everything, everyone; their motives especially. Stopped trusting in people just because I was expected to, because that was what you did. Priests, doctors, politicians... they're all just people, aren't they, at the end of the day? Some of them good and some of them bad, just like the rest of us."

"Were you scared he was going to hurt you?" Susan asked.

Tabby thought for a moment. "I hated him. And he was a monster – a monster in Ireland, and a monster in England. Abusing vulnerable people who came to him for help, who trusted him. So, no, dear, I wasn't scared. Just very, very *angry*."

"So, you're not a nun anymore?" Baker asked her, casually.

"No," she said. "I got... *disillusioned*, you might say. But then, I think perhaps you know how *that* happened."

"How did you find me?" She was irking him, she could feel it; her presence alone getting under his skin. "What is it you want?"

"I didn't find you – you walked into me. And what I *want* is for you to rot in jail for what you've done. But that would affect other people, wouldn't it? Innocent people. So I'm going to have to settle for you stopping... what you're doing here. What you've *been* doing here."

Baker chuckled – but he sounded, she thought, less confident than usual, less self-assured. Smaller, somehow.

"And who are you," he said, "to tell *me* what to do? If you were going to tell someone, you'd have done it already. And if you *have* told someone, they obviously don't care – and why should they?"

"You're killing people. You did it in Ireland, and you're doing it here.

That girl who was 'round here last week, I followed her home. And do you know how I found her, *Doctor*? Dead on the floor, in a pool of her own blood – because of you. You're a drug addict and a psychopath, and you care for nothing and no-one but yourself."

It happened quickly; he was on her in a heartbeat. There was no time even to take a breath before his hands were around her neck, his thumbs pressing into her windpipe. She fell back against the fridge, but somehow managed to stay upright; if she fell, she knew, she'd stand no chance at all. Her hands went to his, trying to peel his fingers back, but it was hopeless: he was strong, much stronger than he'd seemed. She clawed at his face, trying to get purchase on his eyes, but he pressed down harder, choking the life out of her. Her vision darkened, dimmed; she could feel unconsciousness encroaching on her, his spittle on her face as he panted and strained. Her body weakened, and she began to slide down the fridge, which only afforded him more leverage.

Don't go to ground. Fight. You have to fight.

She rallied every last bit of strength she had and pushed herself back up to her full height – surprising him, momentarily loosening his grip. She scraped her nails down his cheek with her left hand, and with her right stretched out to grab the letter opener on the counter. His eyes widened, but he didn't let go, doubling down on the pressure on her throat; so hard now, Tabby thought he might break her neck before she passed out. The pain was excruciating, but she held on, squeezing her fingers around the letter opener's handle, rolling it in her palm. If she dropped it, she'd be dead: it was last simple. With one final surge of effort, she drove it forward, up and under his ribcage. He cried out, but to Tabby's surprise, still wouldn't let go, wouldn't release her.

It didn't work.

She lost her footing, began to fall... but then Baker, too, was dropping to his knees. He removed one hand from her throat and patted his side, as if checking for a lost wallet; inspected his hand for the blood dripping now down his wrist.

Together, they collapsed to the ground.

She gulped in air, great gasps of it. Baker's breathing, though, was laboured – his lungs struggling to keep pace as his heart pumped the blood out of his body and onto the kitchen tiles. It gathered in the grooves between them; spread out across the floor like a red maze.

"P...please," he whimpered. "Please, you can't leave me...like this."

He was on his back now, his words directed to the ceiling. Tabby struggled to her feet and looked down at him: the faces of the women he'd hurt – Ruth, Sinead, Olivia, Belle and the girl whose name she'd never known – flashing one after another before her eyes. She kneeled down beside him, careful to avoid the blood.

"That's exactly what I'm going to do," she told him. "But I want you to know something first. Whatever pain you're in now... you deserve it. Every second of it."

She retrieved the letter opener, wiped it on Baker's shirt, slipped into her coat pocket and walked out of the kitchen.

"Goodbye, Mr. Baker," she said. And didn't look back.

Susan was the first to speak. "Jesus. You just... killed him?"

"Yes," Tabby said, perfectly composed. "I mean, he was alive when I left him, just, but...yes."

Nicole shot a look at Susan, then another at Tabby, unsure of what to say. There was a certain cognitive dissonance to the experience: it was almost impossible to reconcile the story she was hearing with the frail old woman in the nursing home bed.

"And you're sure he died from that?" Susan asked.

"Quite sure, my dear. I read about it in the papers a month or so later. They didn't find him for... well, quite some time. It was the neighbours in the end who, you know...raised the alarm. The articles were vaguer than I might have liked, but they *did* mention a police investigation, though I didn't get the impression they investigated all that hard. There was talk of medical instruments found at the scene, and his history of malpractice was resurrected, of course. I think it was fairly obvious to everyone what he'd been doing in that flat."

"I wonder how long he took to die?" Nicole said. "Not long enough, I'm sure."

"I looked into that a bit, in fact. And it seems there's something like five litres of blood in a man's body. Lose more than 2 litres and you'll die; the body goes into hypovolemic shock, and eventually your organs shut down. His was a small wound, though, so I'd imagine... quite some time"

"Have you told anyone?" Susan seemed to Nicole somewhat satisfied by this last revelation.

"I've told you two." The old woman smiled, briefly. "And two other friends, a good number of years back."

"Would they be two nun friends that visit?" Susan asked. "The nurse that let us in to see you mentioned them. Did they know about Baker, what he was? Or about what happened at Montpellier Street?"

Tabby nodded. "They knew Baker, and that house. And they visit every Saturday, actually. You should come and meet them. They might remember some things from back then that I've forgotten."

"We'd love to," Nicole said, perhaps too eagerly.

"Yes, absolutely," Susan agreed. "Thank you so much for your time. And for sharing your story with us."

"It was strange to hear it out loud again," Tabby said quietly. "It brings back... thoughts, difficult thoughts. Sometimes even your own life is hard to believe, when you look back on it." She paused, considering something. "Tell me, though – should I be expecting the Guards to call at my door?"

"Absolutely not," Nicole told her.

"You just get some rest, Tabby," Susan said. "You've certainly earned it."

CHAPTER 26
2018

"So, yeah," Nicole concluded. "She killed him. Just like that."

"Jesus Christ." Louise put her coffee cup down on the kitchen table and scraped the chair back just far enough to take a seat. "That's mad. Ah, I wish I'd gone with you now. I didn't think it would be so interesting, listening to an old nun..."

"Ex-nun."

"Sorry, listening to an old *ex-nun* reminiscing about her life, but that's a good one— I'd watch that on Netflix." She paused. "She doesn't know where the bodies are buried, then?"

Nicole pulled up a chair of her own. Now she'd finished recounting Tabby's story, she realised, she was a little in awe of the old woman – and more than that, was genuinely looking forward to going back to see her on Saturday.

"Afraid not," she said. "I just can't believe she knew the girls I've seen in the house.

It's just, so sad."

Louise stared at her sister for a second, concerned. "And how are you doing?" she asked. "This has been a lot, I know. Jess dying, then your..."

"Complete break from reality?"

"I wasn't going to say that. Your...struggle. to accept your new reality, I meant. But I really need you to promise me you're going to keep your appointments with Dr Higgins. She's really great, and I know her personally, so I expect you to work with her. And I need you to stay in contact with me. You can get through this, you can – but only if you don't shut us out again. We're here for you, and you know that. You just have to be honest with us."

"I will. I know, I'm sorry. But like I said before, I won't shut you out again."

"And anyway," Louise added, "Susan's here now, and she's very invested."

Nicole sipped her coffee for a moment in silence.

"What?" Louise asked her. "What is it? I can *hear* you thinking."

"I don't want to tell you." Nicole said, sheepish.

"What did we just talk about?"

"I know. But this isn't going to help with those concerns of yours..."

"Nick, what is it?" All trace of her previous good humour leeched from Louise's voice, replaced by steel-edged perturbation.

"I saw Jess." Nicole waited for a reaction, but none was forthcoming, so she continued. "She told me... She told me the girls who died here needed my help. To untether themselves from the house."

"I see." Louise sighed. "When did she come to see you? Because it was only a few days ago that your neighbour rang me to tell me you'd been hoarding meat in your utility room. The same meat you were going to the shop to buy when you and your wife were in the car crash that killed her. Jessica is dead, Nick. So please, tell me: when do you think she came back?"

"This isn't like before, when I saw her in the day," Nicole insisted. "When I...you know. Fuck. When I imagined her. She was a ghost this time, Lou, an actual ghost; she'd come back, just like the other girls did. She was dead, but she'd come back with a message. And to say goodbye."

"So that's it, now? She's gone?" Louise looked briefly thoughtful for a second, as if she'd just remembered something important. "Okay. I've done some reading about this. What you think you saw – it could just have been the rational part of *you* saying goodbye. To Jess, and to... the delusions you'd been having. It could actually be a good thing." Louise smiled encouragingly.

"Fine, doctor," Nicole said, too tired to argue the point. "Whatever you say. But Susan saw ghosts in this house, actually *saw* them... and I'm telling you, Jess came back. Came back and told me I need to go into the basement to help the girls. And that's what I'm going to do, today. Well, it's what Mike's going to do, when he calls 'round. I've been down there and I didn't see anything – we need someone with tools."

"Wait. Mike's going to do *what*?"

"I asked him around to look at the wiring in the basement."

"I see," Louise murmured. "Well... I hope you know what you're getting into. I really do."

Half an hour later, Mike was at the front door with his toolbox. Nicole felt slightly awkward in his company; unsure what Susan might've told him. The last day he'd been at the house, doing the lawns, had been the day Susan had discovered the spoiled meat: the day Nicole's house of cards had come crashing down around her.

"How are things?" he asked her. "You all set to sort out this wiring issue?"

He seemed, to her relief, no different with her than he'd been before. She allowed herself to relax a little.

Yes, she replied. *She was ready.*

"I'll get cracking, then," he said. "See what kind of job it is. No doubt that mother of mine will be 'round shortly."

"There are two fuse boxes," she told him. "One above your head there," she pointed to a space above the front door, "and one down in the basement. And actually, I was hoping we could look down there first, if you don't mind. I thought I smelled burning the other day when I passed by the door."

It was a lie, of course – but she thought it best not to announce her intention to untether the spirits of dead girls from the house so they could rest in peace. And she didn't exactly know what it was she was looking for yet, did she? Only, as Jess had told her, that whatever it was, it was downstairs, in the basement.

"Alright, then. Let's get to it." Mike lumbered away from her along the hall, and towards the basement stairs. As Nicole moved to follow him, Louise appeared at the kitchen door.

"Oh, Mike," Nicole called after him. "Before I forget: this is my big sister, Lou."

"Less of the big," Lou said, elbowing her playfully in the ribs.

"Howarya, Lou?" Mike nodded at the newest addition to the household. "Nice to meet you."

Louise turned to Nicole. "You're going to the basement? I haven't even been down there yet, and you have me utterly creeped out about it."

"Come down with us now, then," Nicole said, trying to give away as little of her own apprehension as possible. "There's nothing in it at the moment, anyway." She tugged at Louise's arm, encouraging her down the steps – and soon enough, all *three* of them were standing in the basement, and Mike was examining the fuse box under the stairs.

"There's nothing obviously dangerous right this second," he said. "But it's really, really old. It'll have to go, I'm afraid, all of it."

"That sounds expensive." Nicole winced a little at the prospect.

"It won't be cheap. But we'll figure something out."

"Is there anything else...unusual?" she asked him, as casually as she could – conscious of Louise rolling her eyes at the request, at her sister's latest flight of fancy.

"Unusual how?" Mike looked around the empty room, confused. "I mean... I suppose it's strange that the whole place is tiled and there's a drain over there in the floor. But there could be a few reasons for that, I guess."

"Right." Irrational though she knew it was, Nicole felt a kind of disappointment wash over her.

"It's a good size, though, isn't it?" Louise said, pacing the basement. "You should definitely find some way to utilise it."

"It's a fine space," Mick agreed. "Should be bigger, though." He cast a glance at the ceiling, then across to the far wall.

Nicole followed his gaze. "Bigger how?"

"That wall at the end," he said, stepping into the centre of the room. "It's been brought in a bit – added after the initial construction, you know? See how it's the only part of the room not tiled, and the tiles joining on to it are chipped?" He ran a hand down the ragged tiling. "Rush job, I reckon – cowboy builders, probably. You've only lost a couple of feet, though."

He tutted under his breath; his professional pride insulted by the shoddy workmanship.

"But why bother moving a wall a couple of feet?" Nicole asked.

"You have me there. I'm not sure, to be honest with you. Maybe it was a supporting wall and they needed to shore it up a bit?" He walked over to the offending wall and gave it a tap with his knuckles; the hollow echo that followed rang out as loud as a church bell across the room. "Well – you can scrap that theory, then. It's only a cheap bit of plasterboard, wouldn't support a feather. Bloody cowboys."

Louise ran her own hand down the wall. "What if there's something behind it? Is that possible?"

"Like what?" Mike laughed – nervously, Nicole thought.

"I don't know," she said, when Louise didn't respond. "Is it something you can check?"

"Check? Like...what do you want me to do, exactly? Rip it down?"

Nicole thought for a moment.

"Yes," she said eventually. "Please."

Mike seemed perplexed; entirely taken aback. "Okay, then," he shrugged

– and ambled back to the place he'd deposited his toolkit, pulled apart the top section of the box and opened it out like he was spreading the wings of a metal butterfly. He moved a few things around inside it, scrutinised an item or two… then pulled out a claw hammer and, swinging it from one enormous fist, returned to the wall.

"You sure about this?" he asked.

"Yes," Nicole said – taking a few steps back, and silently urging Louise to do the same. "Go on – do it."

Louise linked an arm in Nicole's.

"You're holding me pretty firmly for a woman who doesn't think there's anything down here," Nicole said, under her breath. Louise said nothing – but, Nicole noticed, tightened her grip on the arm.

"Here we go, then," Mike told them, and plunged the little hammer into the wall.

The claw went right through the plaster on the first attempt, apparently with little effort on Mike's part. Five strikes later, and he'd created a two-feet-square crater in the wall, at roughly chest height. Nicole grabbed a torch from the toolbox and shone it towards the opening, into the hole – revealing more of those same white tiles, and a space – albeit a small one – that had clearly once been part of the original room.

Mike put down the hammer and began to pull chunks of the wall free with his hands, the plaster causing cloud after tiny cloud of white dust to swirl around their ankles as it hit the ground. At first, or so Nicole thought, there was nothing to see – at least until Mike pulled down a final piece, so low down the wall it was almost at ground level.

"Jesus Christ!" He sprang back, his mouth wide open and his hands splayed out in front of him like a holy man warding off encroaching evil.

"What?" Louise asked him. "What is it? What do you see?"

"There's something in there," he said, the words coming fast, erratic. "Some*one*. I saw a skull – I think it was a skull, anyway. And there's cloth and stuff, like clothes."

Nicole and Louise turned to each other, both equally alarmed.

"We should call the police," Louise said.

"Yeah." Nicole nodded, vigorously. "Can you do it? Can you ring them?"

Louise nodded back at her, then – running, not walking – headed up back the steps to make the call.

Left alone with Mike and whatever he'd uncovered, Nicole moved instinctively towards the hole in the wall. She'd come too far now; she needed to see.

"I wouldn't look, if I were you," he warned her, taking another step backwards.

She ignored him, continuing on to the wall, picking up the hammer he'd discarded on the way. Slowly, she peered into the hole; saw a mass of dirty cloth and, yes – a human skull, just as Mike had said.

They're here, she thought.

In a trance, she raised the hammer and began to chip away at the hole, widening it. Eventually, as Mike had, she relinquished the hammer, using her hands to peel back the larger panels of the flimsy plasterboard, barely cognisant of Louise's footsteps on the stairs as she returned to the basement. The remaining sections spilled out onto the tiles – and with it, the secrets that had lain undisturbed in the wall for the last six decades.

There were at least two skeletons there, laid on top of one other, their clothes mostly intact but faded, worn. The bottom skeleton looked, to Nicole, to have damaged her legs and spine; the bones there were splintered, had never been given a chance to heal.

She flashed back to her conversation with Tabby, to what the old nun had remembered of the worst day of her life and the body of the girl whose death had made it so.

Sinead, Tabby had said. *She jumped out of that window and fell to her death on those very steps.*

There was damage to the skull, too: tiny fractures radiating out across the bone like a spiderweb. Nicole looked down at the remains and felt the grief she'd barely been suppressing rising up in her again, bringing her to tears.

The other body was Olivia's; it had to be. There was no obvious trauma to her skeleton, but Nicole recognised the nightdress immediately; could still make out the embroidered flowers that looped around the hem, exactly like the ones she'd seen on the ghost-girl in the bathroom.

None of them spoke: not Nicole, not Mike, not Louise. Perhaps some things, Nicole thought, existed beyond the limits of what language could contain.

Another something caught her eye: a brown leather shoe, but not one belonging to the first two remains. Olivia wasn't wearing shoes at all – and Sinead's, ragged though they were, were still on her feet. Nicole began to pull away the last remaining plaster board – and, as she'd feared, saw a second brown shoe and the legs of a third skeleton materialise at the edges of her vision. Louise came over to help, and together they pulled away the final piece, revealing the extent of this latest horror. Though it was hard to make sense of what they were seeing, at first.

The newly disturbed dust still swirled at their feet. When it abated, Nicole squinted harder at the hollowed-out wall-space – then cried out, involuntarily.

She was standing, she saw, over the skeletal remains of another woman – and, coiled up inside that woman, as if it had been sleeping in the cavity of her stomach, an unborn baby. A tiny backbone defined the outline of the child's skeleton; its limbs were curved, compressed by the confines of the adult belly that had housed it, but perfect, fully formed. It sat low in what must have been its mother's womb; the mother's bony hand was frozen between her own legs, the left one cupping the skull of the baby who had been, Nicole understood with dawning horror, already making its way out of her body as she lay dying.

Christ.

Once again, she heard Tabby's voice in her head.

Yes, Tabby had said – another of the dead girls had been pregnant. *Due any day then, from what I recall.*

"It's Ruth." Nicole said, to no one in particular.

CHAPTER 27

2018

T he discovery in the basement set in motion a whirlwind of events that Nicole herself had struggled to keep up with.

Mike's first act, on seeing Ruth's body, had been to run next door and alert Susan – who had arrived at the house immediately after two of the Gardai Louise had called. Very soon after *that*, Montpellier Street had transformed into a yellow tape-strewn hive of investigative activity: the coroner studying the remains in the wall, while the forensics team and their cadaver dogs, armed with ground-penetrating radar, searched the gardens and the remainder of the house for other historical crimes, other hidden bodies.

It took six days for them to conclude the search and excavation of the property, during which Nicole and Louise had decamped – with thanks – to Susan's guest bedroom. Twenty-four further sets of remains were uncovered there: a few of them young adults at the time of their death, and the majority of them infants, new-borns. Their findings, of course, made national news – plunging an already-disgraced Church into yet more scandal.

Nicole, though, felt something like relief.

Nicole and Susan kept their promise to visit Tabby again – albeit a week later than they'd originally planned. They'd called ahead this time, adding their names to the official visitor list – precluding any need for Susan to dust off her American accent.

Susan, true to form, brought a big bouquet of flowers.

"You came back," Tabby said – greeting them with a smile. She looked brighter now, Nicole thought, than she had before: sitting up on her bed, her eyes bright.

"How are you feeling?" Nicole asked her.

"Very well, thank you. And very glad you're both here. I've been reading the papers, hearing about what's been going on at Montpellier Street. It was so much worse than any of us could have expected. Which reminds me: my friends should be arriving soon, and I've been looking forward to introducing you all. How have you both been? It must have been very upsetting."

"A little," Nicole admitted.

"Why don't you tell me about it?" Tabby said.

And so Nicole did – told her everything that had happened, the day they found the bodies.

When she'd finished, Tabby shook her head and blessed herself. "May they rest in peace," she said, her eyes glazed over with tears. "They shouldn't have died like that. But I'm glad they've been found and they'll be laid to rest in my lifetime."

"It's a terrible business, though," Susan said. "I can't believe I've been living next door to that for all these years."

Something else was bothering Nicole about Tabby's last statement. "I thought the house was new when you moved in?" she asked. "That you were one of the first to stay in it?"

"Well, yes," Tabby said. "The *house*. But the land itself was owned by the church for decades – long, long before my time. There was an old workhouse there originally, I believe – it was ripped down, and then the land was going to be farmed, but they couldn't get anything to grow on it, so eventually they built the house. I think initially the church intended to sell it, but then Baker took an interest. And it was Father Jameson's house before he, you know... passed away."

"I've been reading all kinds of theories in the papers." Susan looked thoughtful, suddenly. "They say some of the remains could be eighty years old, and some are most likely from the early fifties. But the babies must have been from St. Brigid's. So someone must have moved them. *Then* buried them out the back of number 17."

A heavy silence fell over the room, interrupted only by a knock at the door.

"Hello, hello?"

Two older women entered, not waiting to be invited in: both around Tabby's age, and stooped, though more sprightly, more mobile. One had a head of grey hair while the other was strawberry-blonde.

Tabby's friends, Nicole assumed.

Susan and Nicole rose immediately from their chairs and offered the new arrivals their seats; the women accepted, happily, and settled in for their visit.

"Some new faces in to see you, Tabby?" the strawberry-blonde woman said – her accent oddly reminiscent, to Nicole, of Susan's feigned American drawl.

"These are the ladies I was telling you about last week," Tabby replied.

"Oh, how interesting. We've been looking forward to meeting you two, haven't we?" This last observation the woman directed at her grey-haired companion, who nodded enthusiastically in response.

"I'm Grace," the woman added, extending her hand to Nicole. "And this is my wife, Ellen."

"Grace and Ellen?" Nicole's astonishment, she realised belatedly, was probably written all over her face.

"Yes, dear," Tabby said, with a small laugh. "In the flesh."

"It's lovely to meet you both." Susan offered her own hand, first to Grace and then to Ellen.

"So, you're the one who's been living on Montpellier Street?" Ellen asked Nicole.

"I was," Nicole told her. "And you're the ones who escaped it?"

Grace and Ellen looked at one another and smiled.

"Just about," Grace said. She picked up the newspaper still open on Tabby's bedside table. "We've been reading about the investigation at the house. It was bad there, wasn't it? Worse than we thought."

"It started long before the three of you lived there." Nicole stared at the front page of the newspaper, at the photo below the headline of what used to be her dream home. "Though I don't know if that's any comfort or not."

"Where did you go all these years?" Susan asked the women – unable, Nicole assumed, to contain her curiosity any longer.

"Where did we go?" Grace hesitated; exchanged another glance with her wife. "Canada, in the end. Toronto, specifically. But if you mean, where did we go that day? Then... we just ran. We didn't have a plan or any sort of destination in mind – we just knew we had to get away. I don't know how much Tabby's told you, but Baker wasn't exactly a stable man, and I knew even at sixteen that he'd lost his mind. That he would've killed us if he could've."

She ran a hand through her thinning hair. She looked strong, Nicole thought, despite her age; stoic.

"We knew we had to get out of Galway," she continued. "If we'd tried to get help anywhere in the county, we would've been taken back to St Brigid's, right away. I thought we could maybe hitchhike up to Dublin, somehow... but we had no money, no means. Not a penny to our names."

"How *did* you get out, then?" Susan asked.

Ellen's smile broadened. "We found our guardian angel," she said. "Or, I should say, *she* found *us*."

222

"Ellen, please – we have to keep going."

"But where? Grace, we have no plan. What are we supposed to do?"

It had been two days since they'd made their escape from Montpellier Street. They'd run for only a couple of miles, holing up thereafter in an abandoned barn in an empty field. People would be out looking for them soon enough, Grace was sure; laying low, out of sight, seemed their best and safest option.

She'd got them back on the road that morning, intent on getting them out of Galway – but still very conscious of the need to stick to back roads, to stay hidden. They were still worryingly close to Montpellier Street, to St Brigit's Home; anyone with a car could reach them, easily.

"It doesn't matter where we go," she pleaded, hoping Ellen would listen; would fight back against her exhaustion and get back on her feet. "We just have to keep moving."

Ellen fell into silence. Together, they climbed up the little embankment of the ditch they'd been using to conceal themselves for the last hour, since Ellen's tiredness had brought them to a halt; they couldn't walk in it, not with the mud and water pulling them down, sucking at their ankles like quicksand. When they'd brushed as much of the filth as they could from their shoes and dresses, they began to walk again along the road. They'd need to duck down again, Grace knew, the moment they heard a car approach, which would slow their progress – but better that than they be found and sent back to Montpellier Street. To Baker.

They were desperately hungry, both of them. There'd been water at the barn, and outdoor taps by the farmhouses they'd passed since, but food had been harder to come by. It would be dark soon; the sun was low in the sky, its light fading rapidly.

When, a little while later, they *did* hear a car behind them – the first to have driven past them in hours – it was Ellen who took the initiative, leaping back into the ditch and pulling Grace down with her.

From their hiding place, they listened; waited for the threat to subside.

"It's still there," Ellen whispered, after a minute or two. "I can still hear the engine."

"Me too," Grace said. "Do you think it's stopped?"

Carefully, she climbed the ditch to get a better view of the road, stopping before she could be seen. Sure enough, the car they'd heard had stopped – right in the middle of the road, perhaps twenty feet away from them.

"Stay down," she told Ellen – then saw, to her absolute horror, that the car was now in reverse, moving slowly back towards them.

She slid back down into the ditch, her heart pounding in her chest, and seized Ellen's arm, dragging her up the other side of the slope, where – she hoped – they could make a break for the woodland. The car door slammed; the sound of it startled her and she jumped, losing her footing and sliding back into the muddy water below.

Then, unexpectedly, a voice from the road; a woman's voice.

"Grace? Is that you?"

Grace turned around abruptly and looked up. There, right above them, was Sister Tabby.

"I've been driving around everywhere looking for you," Tabby said. "Come on, get into the car. You need to get dried off or you'll catch your death."

Grace looked to Ellen.

"We're not going back there," she said, hoping she spoke for both of them.

Tabby bent down and offered them her hand. "Good. Neither am I."

"You looked like an angel, when I saw you from that ditch," Grace laughed. "The headlights of the car had you all backlit." She squeezed Tabby's arm.

"You were lucky it was Tabby who found you and not someone else," Nicole said.

The others nodded.

"Where did you go after that?" Susan asked.

Tabby picked up the thread of the story.

"I convinced them to come with me – though you must remember, I didn't really have anywhere to go, either. The convent had been my home, my only home those last few years. In the end, we drove to Ballinasloe; I had a bit of money put aside, so I put the girls on a bus to Dublin. And as you know, I ended up going there myself, a couple of weeks later."

"Tabby's downplaying things a bit," Ellen interjected. "She gave us money for the bus, yes – but also enough for us to get the boat across to England. We worked around Liverpool for the first nine months, and after that we moved on to Canada... and that was where we made our home, our family." She smiled at Tabby. "You saved our lives, you know that. But you also gave us a chance at a new one, too."

There were tears in Grace's eyes. "It would take a hundred lifetimes to repay what Tabby has given us," she said.

Nicole shook her head. "I think all three of you are incredible women. I've only seen what happened in that house second-hand, but the fact you survived, and made a life for yourselves... it's unbelievable."

She was a little emotional herself now, watching the three women together. And sad, too, suddenly: for herself, and for Jessica, and for the women and children who never got out. Whose bodies had been left to rot, away from public view.

CHAPTER 28

2018

"So, what's the plan with the house?" Lou asked.

They were back around the kitchen table at Susan's: she, Nicole and Mick. Susan, meanwhile, was busying herself with an apple tart over by the oven.

"I'm going to sell it to them, I guess," Nicole said. "I mean, what choice do I have, really? It's not like I want to live there, and who else would want to buy the place now?"

The call she'd been expecting had come a few days earlier, from an Irish government employee by the name of Shane Collins – who was acting, he'd explained, on behalf of the department of Housing, Local Government and Heritage. His employers wished, he'd said, to buy 17 Montpellier Street – and were willing to pay considerably more than the value of the property to acquire it.

She'd consider it, she'd told him – whereupon Collins had added, as a kind of caveat, that the offer was contingent on her signing a nondisclosure agreement and, especially, refraining from talking to the press about anything she might have seen, heard or experienced during her time at the house.

What they'd do with the place, Nicole didn't know, though there'd been talk on the news of the building being torn down and a remembrance park constructed where it had stood – and the inevitable promise from the Taoiseach to investigate the history of the house, the girls' home and the church's involvement with both "in a thorough and transparent fashion."

"It might be for the best, selling up," Lou said. "Just... getting it off your hands as soon as possible."

"We'd be sad to see you go, though," Susan added. "We've gotten used to you being about the place, so we have."

"Well, I'm not gone yet," Nicole told them. "Besides... you never know what's coming, do you? I might stick around."

It was strange, being back in the house. The hallway echoed, now the movers had taken most of the furniture – to put into storage, until Nicole had decided what her next move would be. The floors were dirty from the shoes and mud-caked boots of the dozens of people who'd traipsed in and out of the house and the gardens in the preceding weeks. It felt... abandoned, already derelict – though perhaps, Nicole thought, it had never really felt like home.

There was, though, an odd sense of peace now, both within the house and within Nicole herself, as she walked the rooms downstairs, picking up a discarded book here and a photo frame there and loaded them into cardboard boxes by the front door. She didn't go down into the basement; there was nothing there she needed.

She did, however, go *up* the stairs: into the bathroom, where she thought for a moment about Olivia, then on to the small room with the big window beside it, where Sinead had fallen. She looked out through the window, and felt tears prick her eyes.

In her own bedroom, she thought of Belle, and even Father Jameson; a new ghost rushing out at her from every open door. Finally, out on the landing, she was ready to leave – to lock up the house one last time.

Which was when she heard the rocking: the soft knock of wood on wood, drifting down from the attic.

The chair.

She took the pole from of the hot-press and reached up, hooking the attic door and pulling down the folding stairs. She climbed the ladder, the rocking growing louder with every step. And then she smelled it again: talcum powder, vanilla-sweet and cloying in her nostrils.

Her heartbeat accelerated, but still she pulled on the light switch, flooding the room – and the rocking chair at its centre – with artificial yellow.

The chair was empty, its rocking slowing to a stop.

She was alone.

She reached again for the light switch pull-cord – but something caught her eye.

A book, resting on the chair.

She walked over to it; picked up the book, and examined the cover, the title: Terry Pratchett's *Thief of Time.*

Jess's favourite; the one she'd gone to, when she'd needed comforting.

One she wouldn't be needing anymore.

Nicole clutched it to her chest and held it tight.

She'd never see Jessica again, she realised; would never have her back. But nor would Jess be trapped in the house, in its in-between – and for that, at least, she was grateful.

She let out a breath, exhaling the scent of the talcum powder, and switched off the light.

"Goodbye," she told the empty chair, as she left. "I'll see you soon."

When she'd moved back into the house after the accident, it had been with a kind of false joy; something she'd invented, just to survive.

But she left it stronger, more resilient – genuinely hopeful for the future. She'd stay in Ireland, she knew: it was her home now.

She'd be a sister, an aunt, a friend. And – maybe – a partner again. A wife.

But for now, perhaps, it was enough that she *was*.

EPILOGUE

One Year Later

I t was Susan who broke the news of Tabby's death.

"She passed in her sleep," she said, her voice melancholy in Nicole's ear even down a phone line.

It was an upsetting development, Nicole thought, if not an entirely unexpected one. The old nun's health had been poor, the last few months – and, while she and Susan hadn't visited her with quite the frequency of Grace and Ellen, they'd made it out to the care home to see her whenever they could.

"She didn't have any family, did she?" she asked. "Who's going to arrange the funeral?"

"I expect Hawthorn House will have the wake there," Susan said. "And I daresay they'll know what to do about the rest."

"Do Grace and Ellen know?"

Susan paused. "It was them who rang me. They're awful upset about it. I told them they could stay with me for a few nights, to save them travelling back and forth from Kilkee. I was thinking we might have a little get-together in my house after – what do you think?"

"That sounds lovely," Nicole said. "Just let me know what I can do to help."

She'd stayed in Galway, in the end: had rented a property not far from Montpellier Street, close enough for Susan to walk the mile to her new house at least three or four times a week, but not so close that she could pop around unannounced whenever she fancied.

She had lunch every Sunday with Susan and her husband, Billy – and increasingly felt herself part of the Devlin family, the daughter Susan never had.

She was working again, too; had set up her own accounting firm, albeit one she ran from home, and which meant she could sidestep the inevitable stresses of a busy office. She missed Jessica: every day, without exception, she missed her. But she was keeping her appointments with the doctor Lou had recommended, and she answered her phone when it rang. She'd even adopted a dog, for company: a little terrier she'd named Gaspode, who'd given her another reason to get up and out of the house each morning.

Jess, she thought, would probably approve.

The funeral was small, but as pleasant as it could be. A few of Tabby's friends made it over from England, and Grace read the eulogy; she and Tabby, after all, had known each other most of their lives. Grace and Ellen's daughter, Rachael, had flown over from Canada the day before, too – to pay her respects, she said, to the woman who'd saved her mothers' lives, all those years ago.

They reconvened at Susan's house after the service; she'd prepared enough food to feed an army, though there were only about eight people there. After tea and scones, and no small amount of sherry, Grace and Ellen began to regale them with stories from their life in Canada: the campaigning work

Grace had done for women's rights and LGBTQ equality; Ellen's teaching and her social work; the children they'd fostered; and Rachael, the daughter they'd eventually adopted in the '90s, when changes in the law had made it possible for them to do so. They'd been fostering her for almost a year when the adoption came through, they told the group; and though it hadn't been easy taking on a teenager, they were sure – and doubly so, after learning Rachael's parents had kicked her out for being gay – that they were meant to help her.

"She was a bloody nightmare," Grace joked. "We got all the teenage angst and none of the toddler cuteness."

"Hey!" Rachael said, mock-offended. "I was a delight. Some of the time."

When things began to wind down, and the guests began to leave, Nicole went out to the front of the house for some fresh air – and found herself looking over the fence, at the place where number 17 had been.

The council had kept their word, to her surprise, and had levelled the house completely. The black iron fence was gone, a low white wall standing in its stead. They really *had* made a remembrance garden: there was a plaque there now, a memorial, commemorating the women and children whose bodies had been found on the land. There were too few names by far, though; too many girls unnamed, too many infants unidentified.

"You look miles away," Rachael said, appearing at the door beside Nicole. Nicole started.

"Yeah," she said, when she'd recovered herself. "I was just thinking – it's hard to believe it's gone, after everything. All the things that happened there. Though…" She hesitated; smiled. "I guess your parents made it out okay."

"They're pretty amazing," Rachael agreed, returning the smile. "It's funny – they were starting to slow down in Canada, but they seem so much younger here. Maybe it's the sea air."

"Maybe it's being home," Nicole said, quietly.

She could feel Rachael watching her as she stared out at the memorial garden, the remains of the house. "And is this home to you now?" the other woman asked Nicole eventually. "You don't miss Melbourne?"

She let her eyes fall away from the garden. "Sometimes, sure," she said. "But yes, this is home. And you – you plan to stay? Ellen mentioned you might be sticking around."

Rachael nodded. "I think so, if my Moms are. I'd miss them too much, plus I want to be nearby now that they're older. There's not much keeping me in Canada, anyway – I can do my job anywhere. Plus a lot of my friends are dying to visit Ireland. So, yeah... it could be a new adventure for me, I guess. Think the locals will have me?"

"You'll win them over, I'm sure. What is it you do you do for a living?"

"I'm an estate agent."

There were coincidences, Nicole thought, and there were *coincidences*...

"That's funny," she said. "I'm in the market for a new house."

"Yeah? Tell you what, then – you wait for me to get a job, and I'll make sure you get a great deal on your new home."

For the first time since they'd met, Nicole really *looked* at Rachael: the darkness of her eyes, the gentle expressiveness of her face. "It's a deal," she said, and stuck out her hand.

"Done," Rachael responded, and took Nicole's hand in hers.

Her mind on Tabby, Susan rinsed the last of the dishes.

"Everything was lovely," Ellen said, coming over to help her dry. "It was good of you to have us stay, and to lay on this little get-together."

"Oh, don't mention it, dear," Susan told her. "Tabby was a wonderful woman – we couldn't let the day go without giving her a proper goodbye."

Satisfied with their progress on the washing-up, she began to extricate herself from her apron. Halfway over her head, the collar caught on her necklace.

"Let me help," Ellen said, reaching up to disentangle the silver chain from the thread it was snagged on. "Oh, my – that's a very pretty cross." She examined it admiringly, turning it over and over in her hand.

"Thank you." Freed, Susan removed the apron and draped it over the back of a dining chair. "It's Connemara marble. I've had it many a year now – it got slightly damaged before it came to me, but, still... every scar has its tale, does it not?"

Ellen stared at the St. Brigit's cross, running a finger along the fracture. When finally it dawned on her where she'd seen it before, and who it had belonged to, her mouth fell open.

"Where did you get this?" she asked, soft as a whisper.

"It's a bit of a story, actually. Why don't we get the kettle on, and I can tell you all about it?"

"Yes," Ellen said. "Yes, I think we'd better."

THE END

ACKNOWLEDGMENTS

S elf-publishing definitely doesn't mean doing it alone, and I have a lot of people to thank.

Firstly, to everyone reading this, and so hopefully also reading *Awake in the Night:* a massive thank you for taking the time and for supporting an indie book.

A special thank you to Rachael Higgins, who supported and read the book right from the start. She's been a constant cheerleader throughout our decades of friendship - which is why she got not one, but two characters named after her.

Thank you to April Yates for reading an early draft, giving feedback, and reminding me to do my edits.

I'm extremely grateful to Todd Keisling, who provided the cover design and formatting, and to my editor Lynn Love - both of whom really helped to turn my story into a book.

Thank you, lastly, to my partner Nat, who kept everything on track, offered additional edits, and pushed me to get this over the line. I love you.

SHAUNA MC ELENEY is an Irish writer currently based in the UK. *Awake in the Night* is her first novel.

Visit her online at shaunamceleney.com, Twitter @ShaunaMcEleney, and follow her on Instagram @shaunamceleney.writes

Printed in Great Britain
by Amazon

32819855R00134